I0021753

The
Blue Note

The Blue Note

a novel

Translated from the French

Ève Winter

Regent Press
Berkeley, California

Back Cover Collage: Ève Winter
Book Design: Mark Weiman
Translation: Mark Weiman & Lisa Taylor

To Order Books or for Further Information
Contact
REGENT PRESS
regentpress@mindspring.com

Manufactured in the U.S.A.
REGENT PRESS
www.regentpress.net

The verb "to love" is difficult to conjugate: its past is not simple, its present is only indicative, and its future is conditional.

— Jean Cocteau

To all those shade providing trees which embellish my life and give life to my writings.

And also in the memory of Mallarmé.

— Ève Winter

For My Love

PRELUDE

I should not have even been there. I felt overwhelmed with melancholy. This expression is modest by design to soften the pain still present following the recent death of my father. Further, I'd just experienced a series of other traumatic events such as punctuate the life of each of us. It all seemed to be happening at once and every aspect of my existence was affected. In a year my life had been completely rocked. The first person to whom I revealed my pain was a dear friend who I had known for a long time. Wanting to cheer me up she asked me to take her husband's place at an event they had planned to go to together, but which he was not able to attend. This is why I should not have even been there. But then I would have missed another strong and significant experience — an extraordinary love affair.

This affair was such an unique occurrence and so charged with mystery and passion of all kinds that I now indulge myself in relating it, selfishly reliving it and less selfishly sharing it.

I have always been passionately interested in how people communicate. In today's world, although there are still numerous channels of communication, one form has come to dominate — the email or, as we French translate it, *courriel*, for once an elegant gallicism.

I must admit that I have always been skeptical about

this form of exchange, although I don't deny its value and its practicality that has made it so ubiquitous. Yet, of late, my computer has become much more interesting and pleasurable to me.

This man, this character, this human being has come to assume a prominent place in my daily existence. Although we met for only a few hours, and conversed only ten minutes, all evening we looked intensely at each other and literally dived into each others eyes.

Synchronistically, at this very moment, my lover, in a most unusual gesture, sent me a text message (another inspired newly invented form of communication) suggesting that I join him. I replied coolly — rare for me — that I was attending an exceptional evening and could not.

At that time I felt very distant from him. Had he perceived it?

I know I am impulsive and intuitive, but the direction I found myself heading I knew would not prove futile. I was convinced that something important was taking place.

I never experienced such an intense and strong attraction following a first glance. Unlike my usual self I was ready to follow this man right away and go wherever he decided to lead me. I felt somewhat beside myself. It was a strong and strange feeling which inspired me at 5 o'clock the following morning to write a poem that did not reflect my usual poetic style. The words glided onto the page without the guidance of my consciousness. I realized that the style was syncopated and wobbly, as was my sense of time, the vocabulary simple and straightforward. Rereading it now the poem reveals itself as prescient.

PROJECTIONS

An opalescent dawn was fooling around printing on
my languid wall Chinese shadows
The day just welled up
A few birds awakening exhaled some
cheerful trills
An indefinite wave kneaded with desires, turmoil of
life, and immense grief consumed my heart and belly
That morning swelled in mystery
Just a few shared moments but his being overwhelmed me

> *Hallucination of the senses*
> *Fascination of the essence*
> *An illusion intense*
> *An iridescent bubble vanishing suddenly*
> *leaving a disenchanted taste*
> *A still sugary sonata rocked by the moment*
> *radiating passion and forgotten verbs*

Speak the subtle. Ignore the obvious.
Lose oneself in the Chinese shadows and the cheerful thrills
Presents of the beyond-sky

I hesitated to contact him. The decision was in my hands. I had his email address but had not given him mine. My fragile state of mind and spirit of the moment made me hesitant and reluctant to pursue a future connection with him. I was fearful it would lead me on a slope I could not endure. The term "fragile" is somewhat inappropriate, but a different word has not yet been invented to describe my feelings. Three days after our encounter, fearing that he'd soon forget me, I did decide to send him my first email, not imagining that it would unleash a torrential exchange of hundreds.

PIANISSIMO

I provided great detail as to where we had met and myself, really thinking he would have forgotten me and was expecting no response.

And yet...

From: **FB**
To: **Liz**

What a pleasure, Liz, to find you again so fast! I was very sorry for your sudden departure from [. . .]. One does not come across every day an expert on Cicero, Lao Tse, Cervantes and Giraudoux! Do not worry, I believe in your sincerity concerning your language skills. I do look forward to hearing from you soon. Yours, all, dear.

The obviously "excited" playful tone, the last words and also the fact of receiving a response so promptly, seduced me in every sense of the word. So maybe . . . I felt immediately comfortable and confident writing to him. I spoke of myself at greater depth. But the email exchanges quickly took a turn that I didn't prefigure but that I devilishly liked.

From: **FB**
To: **Liz**

But for pity's sake, do not depreciate yourself! You were the only one everyone was looking at [. . .]. I hope you perceived it.

Because of my background — mixed blood of Sicilian aristocracy, Gypsy, and Viking — I am somewhat proud and like to practice the art of repartee with some mordancy. Spurred by the "Do not depreciate yourself" I was looking for a way to convince him otherwise. Unfortunately, however sophisticated the computer may be, it is an imperfect tool. A computer screen reflects thought using a code. It lacks the real depth that only the eyes and the expression may illustrate.

The look . . .

So the idea came to me to replace my words with a vivid picture of myself. My face, reflecting my assurance and self-confidence, was intended to counter "depreciation". The photo I sent was taken right after an extreme emotional shock, the sort of shock that transforms your life and your vision of other human beings. My look in the picture expressed so well what I thought then, "I will survive. I'm stronger and more determined. No one can destroy me."

But I ignored the details of the cut of the dress I was wearing, which revealed my cleavage and enhanced my chest. I sent the photo in response to the first part of his text. The second part of his text also stung me, but I was not unresponsive to it and so much more tolerant.

I realized recently that this black dress definitely has an history since I had purchased it in response to my current lover when he used the word "provocative" to describe the choice of my clothes, stockings and tights. We were in the middle of a chic restaurant, when I slowly and emphatically took off my jacket revealing my cleavage. As I observed his incredulous and ecstatic look at my breasts I dropped, "This is provocation!"

A fewer hours later my computer screen shows . . .

From: **FB**
To: **Liz**

In fact, you deserve photography, and black (and white) suits you so well! You, in words and images, please! Yours, all.

I am very sensitive to subtle language and his play on words won me over as I was wearing a black dress in a black and white picture. This art of verbal finesse thrills me fully. I had doubts about the final formulation though — politeness overused or something special just for me.

Then . . .

From: **FB**
To: **Liz**

I never get tired of contemplating you.

The written compliment has an impact far more potent that the oral compliment, which, as said in cliché, flies away. The written compliment can be read and reread, sipped and savored. It confirms its presence, "But yes, he really said that to me."

While I am used to being courted, and actually it is a game I've mastered — it is not that I mean to brag, it is just the way it is — this was the first time that I had ever been approached via a virtual medium. An immediate response was somehow required, but it was all so abstract. Although the writing was titillating, it was really basically platonic because the looks and gestures that express explicit sexual interest could not be employed.

Sexual interest demonstrated . . .

From: **FB**
To: **Liz**

The insolence of your look immediately conquered me. Not just your look, but that you returned my stare shamelessly. Also, your poise, posture, and sense of self struck me. For pity's sake — Please, please — in your next email, send a head-to-toe photograph. Keep in touch very quickly.

I had proved my point. He recognized my true temperament, which was quite far from "depreciation".

However, I began to be surprised by the extremely accurate insights he was revealing about my personality. He was so certain and I knew he was right. And this after only a week of correspondence. In my opinion, he is a very bright man and has a very refined mind. On top of that he was very intuitive and his intuitions about me were amazing. No doubt, this can all be explained by the fact that he was a talented artist with a heightened sensitivity.

And in spite of myself, docility not actually being one of my characteristics, except with him as I now realize, I considered his request for a full body photo very seriously.

From: **FB**
To: **Liz**

I can understand the euphoria you experience when you stretch and see your own image in the mirror, an experience shared by very few. By the way, why me, who, unlike you, doubts himself? You'll respond to me again, won't you?

And I responded . . .

From: Liz
To: FB

What is it in life that defines an encounter? An exchange of glances? An unspeakable attraction? Multiple answers, but it is wholly mysterious. And it's blissful.

Why you? First, you must know that when I spoke of nobility, what I meant is that for me money, power, fame, neither alienate nor impress me. I love my freedom. I like to agree with myself. I expect nothing. I am seeking nothing. My life is difficult but, unlike many, I feel it is under my control. I don't owe anyone anything and I have respect for myself. A man can touch me only if he touches me. And it matters only that he is the best in my eyes, not in society's eyes. My values are not shared, especially by the majority of women. What have I seen in you? Difficult to define, but still something. You know I do not cheat. I like sharing. I love harmony. Did I feel similarities between us? I barely know you! I liked your delicate insistence. Did I respond satisfactorily to your question?

From: FB
To: Liz

Ideally. We'll change nothing and pursue the exchange. Will you, Liz?

PIANO

To please him suddenly became for me a diktat, and I never rested until my goal to fulfill him was reached. The least of his desires seemed to me important and essential. I had never experienced such a — dare I say the word — feeling of submission. If any one was a rebel woman, I was. I barely understood what was happening to me, except that I was happy to act as I was acting. I was a bit like a caterpillar who prepares her cocoon without any idea of what it was leading to, just by pure instinct.

Nothing else existed for me then but his words and desires. I analyzed nothing about my feelings. I just knew that my indisputably independent self was becoming addicted to everything that he was writing me.

From: **FB**
To: **Liz**

Delicious narcissism! You are beautiful, provocative, in love with your figure — I love this word — an artist, very aware of your seductive capabilities. Black suits you and above all sophistication! I cannot wait to see the fruit of the new photographic session. For who are these pictures made, if not for you and for me. One night at [. . .] for me and for me only you crossed your long legs, made even longer by your pumps. Didn't you? And how much I vibrated. I wait for you . . .

The limits had been exceeded, too much emotion. And above all I did not want to allow him to do so. My rebellious side strung its bow. He was too self assured but also totally truthful. Unacceptable! One cannot be perceived so accurately after only ten emails. Who did he think he was? He was who he was in reality. Too disturbing, so denied. And his choice of words: "for me only; I vibrated; I wait for you." A womanizer to the 10,000th power.

All true, but how to resist . . .

To: Liz
From: FB

Dear, dear Liz,
More than happy to hear from your complex and attractive self. I swear, I will reply amply soon. Yours, all.

To: Liz
From: FB

Dearest Liz,
Please consider yourself an inspiring piece of art, and do accept from a photographer to take advantage of your more than breathtaking figure. Provided she looks at you for what you are, a sensitive person, no doubt the artistic output will be deeply moving.
Answer me whenever you're able to.
Keep in touch.

To: Liz
From: FB

I actually LOVE your words and hints. They require a full and extensive comment. I keep smiling while I read and reread your comments. I keep dreaming as I gaze at your irresistible figure. Let me get back to you at length, as soon as I can spare some extra personal time. Let's keep in close touch.

. . . without a feeling. Nobody before him knew like him . . .

Worse still, the feeling of being naked, body and soul, in between his fingers, in between his words. He has known me since forever ago.

To: Liz
From: FB

Dearest Liz,
It is amazing how far you seem aware and conscious of yourself. And I understand your male relationships haven't been so successful so far. Maybe you impress the miserable ones too much!

So true . . . Or more . . .

To: Liz
From: FB

Liz dear,
Not wrong, your perception of my character. Maybe, we guess each other accurately. You're not provocative, you're just immensely sexy and attractive and lovely, a mere fact the documents you gracefully attached to your last email demonstrate fully.

To: Liz
From: FB

I just got three messages from you: delightful. Your intimate feelings glide through . . .

Again, how to resist the style, the thoughts about us. One of the first times the concept of us, which touches me so much, was raised.

Mezzo Piano

Then were born the first skirmishes which led to an awareness . . .
he cannot disappear.

From: **FB**
To: **Liz**

I thought of you as an utterly independent character: we exchanged glances at first (thank you, Mr. Sinatra!), then words. Was it going too far for you? I would have thought not. But we can come to an early end: just say so, I am not the insisting nasty kind. It's up to you, dear. The best, all the same.

Thus the reconciliation, with a pinprick of humor-truth, which
made me smile . . .

From: **FB**
To: **Liz**

You are the crazy irresistible impulsive kind, you know that. I love it, and your décolleté too, I admit. You CAN NOT blame me for that, can you? By the way, you're some sort of an artist, too. So am I. What's next?

From: **FB**
To: **Liz**

I guess my dreams will all be Liz-obsessed. Let's assume it's a true delight. Your figure is sheer beauty.

From: **FB**
To: **Liz**

I wish I could kiss your smile, to provide me with self assurance and delight. I swear I'll get back to you more extensively as soon as I can. Best thoughts and gestures.

> I'm cracking!!!
> He stirs my heart with his words. Then . . .

From: **Liz**
To: **FB**

The veil of transparent muslin I'm draping my body with will offer you another image of me.
Your writing was again a caress.
Very gently . . .

At this moment of the exchange, although I loved its existence, his sincerity became incidental. To write and to receive an answer or to read and to concoct a rejoinder fulfilled me completely. It vibrated with what I loved most — writing, reading, loving and travelling — either for real or in thought.

One question though, could such thoughts come into being without being crowned by at least a halo of sincerity? To trust and believe in others was so hard for me, and not just with him. No matter. I liked so much what was happening.

From: **FB**
To: **Liz**

Caress, I go for this word you picked up for me. A poem. And a gesture. I care for them both. So do you, dearie.

Yes it is true. I love poems and caresses — to lavish them and to receive them. How does he know that with such an authority? Erotic first exchange, it was fluid under my pen, a term now obsolete, so under my keyboard.

From: **Liz**
To: **FB**

She was a woman and knew instinctively that being female was to transcend the highest difference, the essence of the uniqueness to achieve union.
Highlight the feminine to emerge and fill the masculine.
So her body, from the arch of the feet to the shoulders, was only curves, without doubt likely to provoke the pleasure of caressive hands.
The nails of her toes were varnished — the color of beaches, petals, bird's wings.
Her legs were as she loved — silk, and the iridescent nylons added a layer of softness.
Slightly raised her hips around his soft belly, soft hill providing a perfect hold just suited to hand-caresses.
Her callipygous buttocks so qualified and molded by a sculptor totally crazy about them and crazy about her reinforced the consistency of the curves.
Her waist, moving, was once described as the flexible curve of a musical instrument.
Her breasts crowned with pink areolas formed, like water after a stone is thrown, from the beauty spots to the entirety, all circles.
Even the collarbones ended with two firm small circles.

Her mouth could also boast of being round to promote kissing and sucking.

Her mischievous eyes, painted with mascara, warm color iris rings stretched, however, in a feline look.

Her frivolous soft hair frayed around the prominent corolla — cheekbones round as well.

The world describes as sexy what I allow myself to think as the quintessential difference.

SOTTO VOCE

And appeared the sexual ..

Almost at the very beginning of our correspondence, I, who so love to play and fool with words, ventured, "Vulgarity outrages me." In French, this line would read, "*Le cru m'outre*" which has some of the ugliest sonorities and mismatched terms, that when heard tend to make one smile. And although I designed those words of ungraceful lexicon thinking of them with a strong sincerity, I discovered that vulgarity doesn't outrage me that much if it is accompanied by a draft of tender thought or feeling, like fruity flavor added to a bitter medicine in order to make it easier to swallow. "Boys are spice, girls are sugar, mix them up and you pay the price," as stated by my favorite singer of the moment.

From: **FB**
To: **Liz**

You are magnifique! So singular and intriguing. I'll pack up a bunch of gentle words just for you. Almost forgot: you're the sexiest I can remember and dream of.

Despite the excitement of our correspondence in which we were discovering ourselves both literally and figuratively through our writings and the ultimate conclusion to which they were leading, I wanted still to see the pure form of the beauty of sincerity — honey to remove the bitter taste of the gall. And again and again the sweetness of all this honey, all these bouquets of words, came like so many bouquets of flowers. No man had ever shown me such refined and artful respect.

From: **FB**
To: **Liz**

I saw you at once, sitting with your friend. I dared going and joining you for a chat. I had noticed your figure, your hair, your both amused and curious expression. We talked. Then I did my job, trying to capture your look, which you vouchsafed. I was playing my role just for you, expecting your interest and approval. It came to an end, you had to leave due to your depending upon your friend's car. You were sorry, so was I. I gave you my card. I took your hand. I wished you would remain just with me. But you left, and sent me your first email, almost at once. Then the story went on, still strengthening, ever so romantic and promising. I keep watching you through this machine, the shape of your hardly opened lips, the cleavage of your blouse, the blackness of your eye make up, the enticing way you turn to the artist filming you.

Attractive is a very weak word to describe your outstanding appeal. And I did not have time even to capture a sight of your whole self. Fortunately, photos provide a full view. I dream of your most intimate appearance. Please read my words properly. I wish I could visualize Liz extensively. No doubt one day you'll make this true. While I write, I lose my breath.

From: **FB**
To: **Liz**

I love your unveiling, which I expected and dreamed of as a wishful achievement for you. Because this displaying of your most intimate self fits you closely. Please convey a sample whenever ready! Your cleavage drives me crazy. Yours, all.

From: **FB**
To: **Liz**

None but a confirmation. I know you. By heart. I had guessed it all re your lingerie and addiction for it. You do not dislike Liz. Neither do I . . .

Actually you know me by heart, my love, because you suit me, because I correspond with you, because you carry in you a part of me, because I carry in me a part of you, because we are in balance. That's what I wanted to respond to him. But this vague awareness of a symbiosis that was taking tangible form through our words and that was leading us to a vertigo of union-communion, was . . . too much.

To know and to believe, to believe and to know — interlacing of thoughts that had to ignore reality. There lay the inconsistency. This story, either of love or sex or both, was difficult to achieve. Then I threw a modest and secretive veil to conceal the living future.

Just to seize the instant, to be filled with the other thanks to a sudden-impact meeting, a maze of technology, a write-read, and a conceptual and virtual union. It was already a lot and so rare. Delectable.

DOLCE

The unpleasant bitterness of the drug was softening thanks to the fruity aroma of the divulged feeling.

I wanted him to talk about love and he did . . .

From: FB
To: Liz

Please keep writing and talking and wondering and expressing. I could not imagine that such an emotional flow might stop. And tell me about your feelings about me. It helps a lot. Yours.

From: FB
To: Liz

I love talking/writing to Liz. Something's taking place, stronger and stronger. Let's live it along, intensely. I go to work now, and will get back to you soon. Since you do not sleep, maybe you can answer these words . . .

From: FB
To: Liz

Please receive my best intense feelings.

From: **FB**
To: **Liz**

I'm getting crazy, shivering, unable to speak, feverish, never experienced this so far, getting back to this screen you impersonate, Liz.

During a phone call the night before this email I could notice he did indeed fit this description. The conversation, or rather monologue, was most incoherent. His sentences were chopped and incomprehensible. His words as well. He called me back a few hours later to tell me how he was not himself, and that he never had experienced this before. In fact, he seemed to me extremely capsized. Me too. My heart was beating fast as I was hearing his voice.

From: **FB**
To: **Liz**

Lovely. I love you in black. And in white also. The first photo is ever so sexy, the second ever so tender. This coming new day will be gentle.

So much desire to believe in. So much desire to live. Love is the only emotion that exists. All others are only there to hide it and make it supreme. With my fingers I hid the "lovely" and the "in black" and reread the heat-words over and over again.

But my answer was cryptic . . .

From: **Liz**
To: **FB**

Except to kiss you, which remains in the realm of fantasy and the virtual world of this keyboard, what can I do for you? Also, and please take no offense whatsoever as I speak in all sincerity, but for my part I am not so far along. I could be but I need time and knowledge and above all trust.

In fact, the urge to kiss him remained in me since the first time I caught a glimpse of him. I recently learned that to applaud corresponded to the desire to hug in the literal sense — to take in our arms. It is an impulse born from a desire to show our appreciation of the pleasure the other has provided. I still remember precisely today the pleasure I felt on first seeing him, when he didn't even know that I existed — an irresistible urge to kiss him. When I'm attracted to a man, this is not usually the first thing that comes to my mind. First, I fancy him to notice me, and wait for his signs of attention, and my desires remain mental, not physical as with him.

As for a feeling of confidence, since my childhood I've faced a betrayal of the exposed feeling and I had recently experienced such a violent betrayal of trust that at the moment I could trust no one, not even him. I was like an abused animal that cannot be tamed.

Mezzo Forte

The "What can I do for you?" question contains a modestly worded request. I wanted to go further. I am quite sure that none of this escaped him.

This desire to go further was materialized by him like this . . .

From: FB
To: Liz

Your lingerie haunts my dreams, but your skin and flesh even more.

From: FB
To: Liz

No doubt I would love it all! What a sensuous delight you're offering me, Liz. As well as your charcoal eye lashes. I am pretty sure your intimate drawers contain erotic marvels. You are so... I go back to work with exquisite views in my mind. Maybe next time I will dare plunging into even more intimate confessions and queries. Would you accept them?

From: FB
To: Liz

Liz's secret clue: her most intimate splendor.

From: **FB**
To: **Liz**

Let's share the sweetest, hottest kisses, shall we?

From: **FB**
To: **Liz**

I'm afraid I just love it, and die while waiting to screen the picture, dearest. . . . Please proceed and describe and get me crazy for you.

From: **FB**
To: **Liz**

I am in demand for your descriptions and ambiances. And I feel I could/will please you and fulfil your desire. Because no one before actually felt your character and being and needs like I do. Right? Love.

It could not be more true. Since the first second of our meeting he has had such a deep knowledge of me. I knew perfectly well that he would fulfill me, even though he dared not directly use the indicative grammar tense, a tense which specifically states that — yes he will. We are sure of it, both of us.

More than satisfied. Again and again his words felt so true.

And yet . . .

From: **Liz**
To: **FB**

There are things that cannot be asked because they belong to the now. Then seize the moment or, better, subtly elicit the moment.

And yes ever and so ever the seduction game. . . Lift the

skirt in bits — surreptitiously moistening with the tongue the lips not yet offered — sliding a strap along the shoulder — stroking the hair — all of this to make the computer circuits gulp. From lack of possibility creativity emerges. So words for images, craving for being conquered, craving for more, craving for again. And desiring to seduce — no small challenge since nothing is less attractive than a computer. Photographs — fixed, flat, even though stimulating. Could words have the power to honorably replace all the attitudes, the gestures, and the looks that I knew so well how to use to conquer?

So I dared...

From: **Liz**
To: **FB**

At the crossroads of your long look, I cross my long legs and adjust my nylons.

When during one of our phone conversations he again pleasurably mentioned this evocative gesture that I had wanted to be both physically and semantically sensual, I knew I had again reached my goal.

He was reading me words and soul and I was guessing him impulses and images. Sumptuous exchange, delicious blend. After all, this computer with a silicon heart was conducting our transfer of thoughts very diligently.

Then the *vous* turned into *tu* as a symbol of a connection after an accomplished approach. He was now very close to me. I felt as though I had a physical connection with him. The power of words crystallized. The relationship became intimate. It was he who asked for it, who was the instigator, and once again I was pleased.

From: **Liz**
To: **FB**

Today, I put on makeup and dressed thinking of you . . .
My eyes are black smoked, my eyelashes stiff with mascara and my mouth lipsticked with bright red shiny lip gloss flavored with cherry. I have a new hairdresser. My hair is now very blond, the sun adds its personal touch, and I have stiff bangs that border the edge of my eyelashes. It is hot, I wear my hair up in a capricious bun, letting out a few brown and blond locks which intertwine with my very long pearl punctuated earrings.

Like Brigitte Bardot in the '60s, a black and white mix-short gingham allows my legs to enjoy the caress of the sun. Behind the small buttons of my blouse, my red bra, the kind that corset makers call "Push", can be subtly seen. My waist is narrow and gives full curve to my hips. My shoes are red too and their wedge style causes my feet to arch with elegance.

I walk with a swaying and rolling gait. I feel sensual with all this honey-sun. The caress of your desire burgeons in me and leaves me in a wave of incompleteness. Behind huge black sunglasses that eat my face my mind wanders. My sweet scent is released into secret corners, but rebels as no one is there to inhale it and become inebriated.

I would like so much that you devour me as one of your books, the imagining and the writing of which made you passionate and transcendent. Let your irises dilate with pleasure in front of the blown words and images just like in front of my body ready for love. Let your eager fingers run through my whole body with the same zeal for discovery and sensual perception. Let the ink and the softness of printed pages merge with your senses and with my perfume and the sweetness of my skin. Let the emotion aroused by the words metamorphose into thoughts, drown in bliss in the anticipation of pleasure born first in your mind. Let your spiritual and physical enjoyments join, provoked and dictated by

*me. That once you turn the last page you will feel as fulfilled and
enriched by the Reading as you would by the Liz-effect.*

*Under the unique eye of the photographer
I wear "Diamants Noirs" perfume by Armani
black suede shoes with vertiginous heels
a scarf the one I wore at the Louvre pyramid
it wraps voluptuously around my neck
down my throat and punctuates the top of my thighs while I lay
languid in the middle of my white leather armchair.*

*Under the flash of shameless zoom camera
I wear "Ma Dame" perfume by Jean-Paul Gaultier
a black cashmere v-notched sweater
black pumps with skyscraper heels, cut into strips
and closed with little buttons.
I lie down on the bed, replace the pillows,
go against the current and form a right angle
stretch and cross my legs along the Arabic latticework that serves
as a headbord.*

To be continued only if you like.

FORTE

pparently he loved and longed for more and better. He wanted to go further and deeper into me . . . It was predictable, expected, but what was unexpected is the fact that I found an intense pleasure while trying to escape a primitive vulgarity. But I understood later on that the truth and authenticity, in short sincerity, cloaks vulgarity with the most elegant dress which then no longer appears as such but as sublimated eroticism.

These words, which were part of "the crude that outrages me," did not initially prove exciting to me. The only American lover I had known was my husband and he wasn't very loquacious. I had more written and oral exchanges with the last two men in my life in one year than I had in nine and a half years of marriage. Consequently, my erotic vocabulary in English was very poor. Then I discovered its potential and it made me much more aroused.

From: **FB**
To: **Liz**

Darlingest, Please do not worry too much about your age. A fact is that you are superb, sexy, attractive. Different in a word. Who would care about your date of birth? I don't, no one does. I feel your self esteem utterly basic for you, not only your beauty, your behavior also, so demanding. No doubt

one has to raise to your level. What a redeeming! I love your descriptions of those photographed love scenes, I dream of those you'll work out just for me. Yes, do check your black stockings, show your so high heeled stilettos, lift your tight skirt, rub your full breasts, open your purple lips, stroke your exquisite pussy (since it is a concealed secret of beauty, is it not?) I am proud, so proud to please you. My mind, my spirit, my body, my cock. Loving thoughts, dreams, expectations.

My first reading was swift and eager. On the second reading I was stopped by the words "stroke", "pussy" and "cock". My third reading clung to the words "Darlingest", "secret of beauty", "so proud to please you", and especially the last sentence. Without me asking for it, he knew how to artistically mix sex and love. (Long experience? Delicate charmer? A gentleman in the soul? First try not too brutal?) He did it just like I like it so I could not only accept it, but enjoy and appreciate it.

In fact, I was very moved by this first long text transgression into the sexual domain, text that said he was listening and caring. He had the sensitivity to initially mention my concerns, then he shared with me what was happening in his head. I expected that, of course, but confirmation is always nice. Finally, I caught his insecurity about his power of seduction. Insecurity absolutely confirmed by the order chosen for his path of seduction. First his intellect, then his body and finally his sex. Very clever idea to keep sex last so it is remembered better. I was also absolutely sure that he excelled in the field.

He did not then know how the admission of this insecurity affected me. For my part, I have never doubted my powers of seduction, men having eyed me since I was twelve. So we complemented each other, and we tacitly understood each other.

Obviously I was seduced by his intellect, but what he did not realize is that so many details of his appearance went straight to my heart — his brown hair which flowed in long rebellious locks down his neck, his luminous and unexpected smile, his hands which I found beautiful, his features reflecting pain, the shape of his mouth, something else also, indefinable, and his overall look was alluring. In short I was really attracted to him.

Then my rebellious character which I never lose took hold. I will give ground, but not so easily. For sure, you could not use that stupid expression "easy woman" to describe me. I have expressed that "in order for a man to touch me, he must first touch me". I cannot be more exact. Very few have achieved this, and he soon became conscious that my bar is high.

Thus ensued the following response . . .

From: **Liz**
To: **FB**

I'm an extremely feminine woman. No doubt you have seen this clearly. This implies a clever and subtle balance between sentimentality and sexuality (you wrote sweetest before hottest — I like that) that are not necessarily in the male brain. In my case, being a very complex human being, this equilibrium can break easily, so choose well your words. "Crude outrages me" do not forget. Nonetheless the very civilized brain has a valve for it. In your last email, I read between your lines that what you really want, beyond my own intimate descriptions, is being able to tell me about yours. So I respect this fact. You take the risk that you will disturb my vision of you. You may not worry about it. But I want to subtly perceive you and collect your fine deepness.

A word about me: I love so much to make sophisticated love like you, so much so that my privacy is constantly crying with loneliness . . . for the moment. I love chatting with you this way and I want it to last . . .

Then came his answer . . .

From: **FB**
To: **Liz**

You wrote you wanted me to express my feelings and desires. I do so, since, in a way, I know you love it too. No claim to shock you. But what could be shocking provided it is sincere, deeply perceived and shared? With you, I feel free to write love words, and not ashamed at all to quote my admiration and dedication for your beauty. You are not your sole body: could you imagine I did not get the essence of your being? Could I plunge right into your heart and sex if I had not captured the truth about Liz? You are a lover that has not been loved accordingly. *A Delicate Balance.* **Do you remember this play by Edward Albee?**

Still this great difficulty trusting. Yet his words touch me so much! His arrow reached the center of an essential truth about me. In a few sentences he summed up precisely what I was about, what was my essential truth. I was fascinated by this ultra vision. He had a feline-night and eagle-day eye. He had a supernatural side which brought wonderment to my eyes.

So . . .
How To Have A Love Affair Through A Computer?

I was so tired of all the difficulties in my life that had accumulated and put such a muddy screen in front of the pleasures that life could still offer me, that I decided to dive and snorkel, body and soul, into this relationship that felt so good to me, but, as experience had implicitly shown me, could be devastating. I knew I had the power to decide that whatever was going to happen, I would get from this love affair only pleasure to soothe my wounds and I promised myself that even if the suffering were to come, I would have the power to ignore it.

I respect myself and know I am capable of such determination. I had already experienced such pain that I knew the rules. So I decided finally to go for it and to fulfill all his requests, in which I took great pleasure, even if there was a bill to pay.

Then...

From: **Liz**
To: **FB**

I do not know the play you mention, but I will discover it. I like your answer and I send you my sweetest kisses. Feel free with me, you're healing me.

From: **FB**
To: **Liz**

Your sweetest kisses reached my inner self. I loved their taste, their depth, their unending wilderness and demand. They plunge into my throat, my spine, my heart, they drive my conscience to obsession. My body is set afire, my cock hurts, begging for your attention. Lovesickness.

Never had a man written to me like this, the most precious present that exists, which filled me with tears of emotion.

From: **FB**
To: **Liz**

Tell me about your intimacy, I'm addicted to your self descriptions. Then, if you care for it, I will tell you about me.

From: **FB**
To: **Liz**

Can you believe I actually see you, see through your most intimate pieces of garment? Due to a single glimpse in [...], to a bunch of pictures, to thousands of those words and thoughts we've kept exchanging for almost two months now. Of course I feel the honey taste of your mouth, the firmness of your nipples getting bigger and bigger, harder and harder under my kisses, the shape, the color of your most concealed hair bush: O Liz, please plunge deep into your most passionate inspiration to paint your secretive self for me! As I write to you, my body is erupting, desperately longing for your love art and ability. You're such a ravaging poetic beauty!

This led me to my turn to make him an offering . . .

From: **Liz**
To: **FB**

In keeping with the tonal nuances of clothing worn, black and white are opposed, white silk skin and black foaming fleece. Triangulated heart at the top of my thighs, beautifully designed without need of modification. Between two hillsides bursting with desire proudly stands this small piece of flesh, that little piece of me that creates the thousands of waves so sweet to my belly. Before your eyes will wander to this narrow valley covered with dew, a delightful moisture that glides on the fingers . . . Satisfied?

From: **FB**
To: **Liz**

Overwhelmed.

Never before had I provided such a description of myself. I

even used a mirror to make the description more accurate. I did it just for him, to satisfy him fully, and I took great pleasure in doing so.

Since beginning this novel, I've been searching in vain for a term that could replace the word "pleasure". None of the words I've come up have any graciousness to my senses. Pleasure had not been part of my vocabulary, or my life, for such a long time with such realism.

From: **FB**
To: **Liz**

My wonderful Liz,
I have no breath, no words yet to answer your erotic poem. And I'm attending a very serious seminar (seminar=semen, mine for you). I will get back to you ASAP. Yours, all.

Again and again this gift from him. I take in all its integral wholeness everything he wants to offer me.

FORTISSIMO

From: **FB**
To: **Liz**

Never did I inspire and receive such a poetic and accurate account of someone's intimacy. My feeling is that your pussy is the most accomplished and splendid part of yourself. It is a compendium of Liz's achievements, both utterly natural and untrimmed, as well as sophisticated and so sensual. It provides visual and sexual delight to the fortunate one you agree as your lover, not many indeed compared to the number of applicants. I dare figuring myself as the one to come. The one to whom you will allow and expect he will lift your dress, kiss your skin with passion, stare at your eyes, place his hand on your sacred bush, his lips on your inner lips, his tongue around your erected peak and swallow your spirited liquor. You make someone else of me, Liz. I take you to [...], deep in my heart and cock. Yours, wholly.

Successful. He clearly announced that he had perceived my intimate description as I wanted him and, more importantly, that he would be my lover and how. I admit that his words touched me a lot, alas only virtually. I wanted so that he would really touch me. The fact that he thought about my satisfaction, without mentioning his, touched me deeply as well.

I asked myself questions about his sex life since I had made someone else of him. I could sense why I made him different, but wasn't able to read the writing in his eyes.

I adored that he mixed sex and love at the end of his letter. And the fact that he was giving himself wholly to me made me dream.

From: **FB**
To: **Liz**

Never heard of such a love story, but obsessed with deadly lust and ever growing desire for you, Liz. My whole body aches, you only could provide relief, you know how to so well. One more guess, this time I know I'm right too: as far as love making is concerned, you are an artist, aren't you? The rim of my cock to stroke gently your eye lids and lashes...

The tone was set: unleash the full erotic fertile imagination with which we were both filled. And I found a lot of pleasure because before touching my body, his words went through my mind. It was a double pleasure like no other since. When you make love in reality, action takes precedence over words. Also, in real life we cannot savor words so much because they are oral, immediate and volatile. We talk to each other and we excite each other before and during sex, but it leaves a taste of transience. On the contrary, his written words belonged to me. They were my slaves that I could enjoy as I pleased. They were offered to me like a meal for my senses and my mind for all eternity. And so it went on and on, the same act described always with different words, becoming stronger and stronger, and more and more extreme but still not reaching the limit because of the frustration of not actually living it. Sublime pleasure of voluptuousness. No surprise that we being poor fleshy humans succumbed so abysmally at our second meeting. And I am grateful that night to fate that a needed ride, and above all respect for friendship, kept us from succumbing at our first meeting. Everything would have been so different if we had.

From: **FB**
To: **Liz**

Don't you worry, you're not leaving my mind, my heart, my body. Sweet and wet dreams, you my over sexy vision.

From: **FB**
To: **Liz**

Well done! How could I concentrate on my work with your half naked image before my eyes? I have always seen you as a love lover and expert. I try and imagine your most daring gesture and postures, because you are the most unashamed and altogether delicate person I've ever met. Your curves, your ankles, your ass, your wrists: frailty and fullness. For me I'm all slim and sex.

Why is this man so precious to me. Through a few words and a few photos he was able to perceive me absolutely as I am. For me it is magical. Before him, no man had been able to go beyond my appearance as he did. No doubt then that my affection for him would be violent. He knew how to see my dualities, both physical and moral. He knew how to read in the depths of my soul. I hoped this ability was engendered by love and not by a sharp professional or personal competence in reading people. I kept my joker card of doubt to myself.

As for me, I have mastered the art of extrapolating beyond the concrete and I knew exactly, and without any doubt, how he was built physically and sexually.

From: **FB**
To: **Liz**

You are a magnificent person, just notice all men's attraction to you. Take yourself for what you are, for I viewed you at once. A lovable love loving female with obvious instincts. I was younger once, too, but never felt so powerful and sexy, since I was able to drag your attention. I wish you could see me while I write to you: I am sure you would feel and view and enjoy how horny I am just for you. Fairly indecent and conspicuous: you love it, don't you? I can almost feel your nails and lips on my essential self. Once more you love it, Liz, don't you?

Of course I love it. I loved it. I will love it. I would loved it. I would have loved it. I would have had loved it. The French language induces feelings by the tenses mentioned. It is a subtle linguistic supremacy.

Always the questions reflect his insecurity, his need for me to reassure him. It is also a clever tactic. It makes me think twice about his desires and consequently I come about to his way of thinking, being persuaded that we are on the same track. In fact, he handles his words so well that they serve in their absoluteness to marry his will to his desire. His descriptions are nectar to me. He's again mixing love and sex. I find this very touching, like an arrow going directly to the center of my heart. He knows how.

Yes I like sex and every time it is a pleasure and delight for me to have both the power to cause an erection and to exploit all the enjoyment that can be gotten from it.

From: **FB**
To: **Liz**

Do not change in any respect, please! I love you the way you are,

in every aspect. I hold your breasts to my lips, kiss and bite the nipples, cover them with shining fluid, stroke them with the rim of my demanding cock. Your long red painted nailed hand holds it, presses it between your breasts, takes it to your lips and tongue . . . I almost faint with delight. Would you?

So direct, so exclamatory, so coming from the heart. The two first sentences make me fly away. I want to believe that he loves me for real. Regarding the program that he is proposing, I don't see anything else more tempting. Pregnant imagination. I can feel the softness and the pressure of his lips, the brushing of his tongue on my nipples standing erect towards his mouth. Diffuse pleasure. The head of his cock on the tip of my breasts. I want it now. I feel a boring in the depth of my belly. I want him to faint with delight when my mouth will grab his cock, stopping by furtive and pressed touches. When my wet tongue, my discreet teeth, my raping eyes, will indulge in absolutely all he is expecting from me. A voluptuousness that he never experienced that only I know how to lavish on him. Woman instinct only for him.

From: **FB**
To: **Liz**

How do you expect me to concentrate when you send to me the most staggering of all the photos of you that I have seen? This one is really devastating sex-appeal — your lingerie. O this red bra, those black nylons, and garters, this exquisite skirt! Jumpsuit. One of my favorite attires. This scarlet ribbon, the tempting expression of your face made up like I love. Your lips. Your eyes. You have to tell me the story of this picture which has nothing innocent. Who conceived it? Which wardrobe? Bought where and when? In which circumstances? For whom? You are beautiful in this sophisticated pose of a saloon girl Liz. Your cleavage cannot leave anybody indifferent. Above all, if, like me (only me?) we get the shape, the volume, and the heaviness crowned by the most voluptuous nipples that exist . . .

I loved making him completely crazy about me and also perceiving in him an ounce of jealousy. It became a game. I chose from all my sexy and erotic pictures those that seemed most suitable to excite him, to make him desire me with obsession. I wanted to push the game to its most extreme, feeling protected by the computer screen, and thus allowed to reach the superlativeness of this love affair. I wanted to maintain him in this state of excitement without any ending, leading to a frustration that would supremely overflow the first time we would make love. It was so unique. I read somewhere that "The best time is when you are waiting". Well, in our case this waiting was prolonged, creating an exceptional voluptuousness which is what I wanted.

From:	FB
To:	Liz

I'm desperate. I wrote to you the hottest lovingest ravagingest letter I ever thought of, so daring I was not certain not to shock you. Wrong feeling, nothing regarding passion could hurt you, is it not? I described the perceived splendor and proudness of your tits, I could but just imagine under your garment when we met, but which you offered me on the first picture you sent me. I said I would love them by gestures, licking and biting the erected fleshy nipples, gently and hardly covering them with shining fluid, making you come and scream when I'd rub my too big burning sex upon them. I described my almost fainting with joy when you confessed you had fallen in love with me and my cock, sucking it with so much expertise and intuition it looked like an artistic creation. Because your love making is pure art, I'm sure, and we'd make photos of it, so as to get even more crazy for one another. I realized I had never used my imagination, fantasy, day dreams to such an extent. I could not do anything but wait for your answers. Expecting you would go on in this daring style, which I promised I'd share if you wanted me to. Will you?

I could initially intuitively feel the truth of his words, but I also noticed some mistakes, rare for him, which I suspected betrayed his confusion generated by the narrative. Also, being prone to doubt, I couldn't accept my initial intuition, and was puzzled why I had not received his passionate and daring love letters. He was right again, though, concerning our correspondence. He knew that I would like to share with him the daring style we were developing because, once again, we like the same things.

From: **FB**
To: **Liz**

I think of you, despair/distress, my whole self thrills with impatience. I let you open your thighs and string for my greedy lips. My vision just at this moment: your long nailed painted fingers pulling aside your drenched string, gently stroking your burning pussy.

From: **FB**
To: **Liz**

Your love meal drives me crazy (that's why you cooked it just for me!). I long for your five-courses feast. I'd like you to concentrate on each of them. Your mascara painted eyes, and what you would do with them. Your red wet glossy mouth, your expert tongue and teeth. Your triumphant boobs, their

nipples oversized with lust. Your slim waist, circled with an outrageous garter belt and black lace panty. Your divinely long shaped legs, with their over tensed brown black stockings. Your round, firm, soft ass, just made for my hand and mouth. Your most attractive self, your cream filled love pussy, hardly covered or discovered by your dark string, showing your shining fur and opened purple lips. A full description of each of those love tools, and how you would play with them and me. Then, I will tell you about my own body, but not before you tell me how you perceive it. You saw my face, my hands, nothing else. But I am sure you guessed the rest, including the most intimate and protrusive . . .

No man had ever dared to write me in such specific detail and vocabulary. So I learned to read, understand, envision, appreciate, and to wait again and again and, to soften things a bit, become exhilarated by his unique way of talking to me about sex.

I am very adaptable and have an insatiable curiosity, but not an unhealthy one, about all living things. I learned early on that wearing blinders, setting limits, and accepting the perceptions defined by others was not my cup of tea. A bit for a wild horse.

I expected from him the utmost in feelings and surprises. I wanted to discover a land with him where there was no hurt, but only the best well-being that exists. However, when sentiment gets involved with sex, it can be devastating. It is true, but at this time my brain ignored all negative thoughts in order to be happy.

He succeeded. I developed an immeasurable and uncontrollable desire for him.

My sex was calling him with all its might . . .

From: **Liz**
To: **FB**

F. (Stage direction: "sensually whisper his name so that all his senses shiver") when you will discover my underwear, specially thought of and selected for your pleasure and for you and only for you, it will murmur to you the proper gesture and nothing else will exist for me than the word softness, whose sonorities are already sparkling and sweet. Softness of your eyes, your eyelashes, your hands, your mouth, your lips, your sex, your words, your gestures, your ultimate caress.

From: **Liz**
To: **FB**

In between your fingers I want to become the highest concept of a woman. I want to become the woman who lurks in the depth of my soul that only you know how to create. "Lick me, suck me, drink me, penetrate me, caress me, get me drunk with the intoxicating liquor of your manhood until I faint. Make love to me paying attention to all my ways of coming. You have to learn me. I allow you absolutely all that will fulfill you. Although I know in advance all you love. Write to me again all the fantasies you will like to share. You make me come without preconditions. I love your words so much. In expectation of our essences mingling, it seems like our emails are also intertwining.

From: **Liz**
To: **FB**

My tongue and my lips, silk and velvet, graze where you want. I feel like I need your hands and your mouth all over my body, need to feel you in me, need you to take me over and over, need to be on top of you so that you may penetrate me deeper. I need to fill all your desires. I will take you in my mouth, caressing you with my tongue, my lips, my teeth right where I know you love it, while my nails will be present at the most sensitive of your tender spots. F. I want you so much.

I always made a distinction between the desire and the need, one being the paroxysmal form of the other. With him I should have written, "I need you." But that would have led to an obtuse spiral and would have been an iridescent reflection of the thought behind those words.

And yet . . .

From: Liz
To: FB

I want you to savor me slowly and enter the climax of our desire, despite my pleas.
Let our limbs intertwine producing soft, mouth-melting, mouth-pulsating passion.
I'm creating an atmosphere so that our senses will be heightened and filled — Dim light, in order for you to see all you want to see of me, a transparent and light-reflected rainbow on my skin.
Taste of us, taste of me (actually almond), strong alcohol taste (literally and figuratively) on your lips, on our mouths, in our mouths.
Sensual Blues caresses and tickles our ears. Silk, lace, chiffon, and erect nipples. Delicate and particular scent of lust. I have the maturity and experience to be like this today. I had a lot of misery, but now I've learned to choose appropriately. The chaff is discarded. Only the truth remains. I maintain a true integrity and I am an Epicurean. Concerning love, you have to know that I am integral to the end of the scream.
Conquer me with your eyes, your lips, your hands, your sex, your voice, your art, your passion your words, your supremacy and

your brilliance.

As for me, I offer to you my prettiness, my art of love, my languages, my softness, my differences, my unpredictability and my mysteries.

I kiss your hot lips and whisper in your ear, "Lick me."

Close your eyes, let my hands caress your body and provide a fabulous Japanese massage which is my secret. Follow your chills and waves of desire that overwhelm you with each pass of my soft and caressing fingers — on your face, your neck, your chest, your sex.

Let your mind wander to a carefree land, give yourself to me with emphasis and confidence.

Your eyes are still closed and your flesh intoxicated with desire. Then my lips like butterflies, my eyelashes like hummingbird feathers, take over from my hands which nestle somewhere on you. My mouth becomes tender and kisses your eyelids, bringing freshness and languor to your thoughts. On your cheek my eyelashes love your skin and cuddle it. My lips go down to your ear and whisper to you unbridled ideas. They are filled with a desire to discover an unknown territory, venturing everywhere and finding an anchor standing in their path. They dock there. My tongue is inventive and tastes all of you, licking your sex at will. Tea ceremony after the Japanese massage. I welcome your pleasure when it wants to bloom all over my body. Sleep well my love.

I never before opened my heart, my feelings, or my body this way. A voluptuous swirl inspired and imposed by him. I felt good in this symbiosis. For his part, I knew he felt exactly the same way. Miracle of technology — my words would reach him almost instantly and he would answer me, so we were allowed to say anything, expressing the entrails of our feelings without a veil because the screen allowed the depths of the depths to emerge.

We are pioneers of this erotic correspondence which pushes away all boundaries. He is a talented writer who excels at it. The need to share this correspondence imposed itself strongly on me. I felt I must testify about this new technological phenomena which had such unexpected and unforeseen consequences when put in the hands of a sexual, emotional and literary genius. It is an art to transform a practical technological device into an inventive media to communicate epidermal sensuality. We are apprentice sorcerers experiencing the magic of this new kind of exchange and our love, hesitating between virtual and real, drew strength and nourishment from it.

FLASHBACK TO THE FUTURE
FIRST BREAK

When we met he told me that those pictures I'd sent to him, especially the first one, looked as if I were saying, "Fuck me. I'm here. Look at me." These are his own words.

I have already explained at length why I sent this first photo, but I'm writing this book in order to expose every detail of this part of my life and to reveal everything. So it is obvious that only an accent of sincerity dictates my narration. After all, it is possible that his interpretation reflects some truth. He knows so well how to read me with all the nuances that this process entails. Maybe, unconsciously, that's indeed what I did mean.

Considering everything, and after shaking off the Judeo-Christian morality that soaks our education and leaves us open to feelings of guilt, I declare, "Why not and so what?"

Life has mistreated me, so to punish it I drink it to the full. I fear nothing and nobody. I know in advance what life is reserving for me — to take away from me all those I love. Even my cat that I adore and miss so much. So, I prepare myself with temerity. It has been this way ineluctably since I was born. But since he became a presence in my life, I henceforth determined to tie my future love.

Yes. I love love. Overall, I like to make love and I'm made for it. At least this is one intense pleasure that I can steal from this sometimes all too sour existence. Moreover, he shared with me this quote, "If god created something better, he kept it for himself." This quote is quite pertinent to me.

I have had, with one exception, all the men I desired and I regret absolutely nothing.

My heart, kneaded with tenderness and very welcoming, scratched a little bit every time. But it still beats and beats even stronger. And, some of these men, despite their absence and distance, still frolic in my heart, kneaded with tenderness and very welcoming.

I refuse to live on a dance floor where the rhythm of the music hinders the expression of my inner self and with a pianist who bridles my eclectic musical tastes. Maybe one day a man will know how to tame me.

Meanwhile, I want to gorge myself on life and give myself the very best. And when life points its mean snout at me, it multiples my energy and makes me want to show to life who it is dealing with. Although my social status doesn't predispose me to it, I am in touch with many notable and famous people. I have had entry into the presidential box at the French Comedy in Paris. The top General of the Israeli Army, a really very handsome man, asked me to marry him. At the moment, I live in the richest state in the world. Robert Redford had a crush on me and, amused by my name, asked for a photo to be taken of the two of us. My pictures appeared in a prestigious Italian fashion magazine where I was wearing clothes from the 1940s. I travel first class and have a chauffeur-driven limousine waiting for me at the airport. I stay at the most beautiful hotels and spas and eat at the best restaurants. In short, all of this in order to demonstrate that a persevering lust for life is rewarding. Mediocrity and baseness outrage me and I avoid them whenever possible. No need then to specify that no act of baseness was the source of all these advantages. I received them because of the circumstances and because of my explosive sincerity and my own specific and uncorrupted way of approaching life.

The fact is that if, and only if I insist, this picture seemed to say to him — "Fuck me. I'm here. Look at me." — literally he did fuck me very well (risque terminology that I am borrowing). Even if it means to tousle the moralists, in his shoes, I would also have picked up the flower that opens on my way in order to admire it while it lasts. And, even if it means to walk on his same path and wavelength, I had, for myself, dazzled and conquered a star and basked in his aura, the time lasting like a shower of shooting stars in summer.

Tied...

COMING BACK TO THE
PRESENT
SECOND OFFBEAT

I t is absolutely out of the question to compare. It is pointless and bleak. However, I would like to mention his peculiarities, things which belong to him alone. Of course, coming from my own feelings and experiences, with all their empirical and personal implications, it is a restricted and limited reality. A reality just for me and for my eyes.

Is it possible to discuss specific features that only exist in relation to other features? I am going to try to express it, remaining faithful to what we lived.

So, if I look at this story from above, my perspective being on a global level, it would appear to me as an exercise in style full of sophistication and transcendence. It is evidenced by the words chosen for the match, the conditions and locations of two meetings — the first and the last — the phrases exchanged, the moments of intimacy, and finally acts of love and the words spoken during sex. However, I leave space for spontaneity and sincerity, undeniable from my point of view at least. It was already a marriage of desire and impromptu that made the adventure sparkling, an adventure that was technologically prepared a few months beforehand.

I do not pretend to have extensive sexual experience because of numerous lovers — although everyone has a different idea of what constitutes numerous, especially in this area. I am average . . . for a male admittedly. My peculiarity is that my lovers are widely various, cultural diverse and generationally disparate. It is my sharp sense of observation of details and my very aware sensibilities that forged me into the lover that I am, not unbridled numbers of sexual partners.

Every man has his own way of making love. It fulfills me. I hate routine. I loved his way.

My lovers are generally younger than me, sometimes much younger than he was but I discovered a new concept with him — a form of worship, sophistication and expertise. I've known crazy love, passion, and paroxysmal desire, but not really worship. He knew how, by his words and actions, to make me valuable and rare. Like a wild pearl.

He was never inhibited by decency and the unsaid. He always expressed what he saw and thought without taboo. He expressed naturally what he thought and felt and I savored it, always with the most evocative and fearless vocabulary. He had a subtle and delicate intelligence with words that made him seem like a unique jewel to me. I experienced an intellectual and physical pleasure with him. Connivance of body and mind. His exacerbated sensibility and sensuality are the reflection of his inner self. Some of his caresses and some of his words will remain forever in my secret recesses.

I think I know him better than anybody else in his intimate depths and his profound being, despite all the despites.

HISTORY OF A SUITCASE
THIRD MARKER

I was bought because more beautiful than the others. Always this need of perfection, flattering but extremely expensive. She allowed herself a lot of indulgences. She's going to eat pasta. Well done for her. She really doesn't have to be quite so chi-chi for him and his desire for "frills" (like he said) ... this is not my expression, but his ...

Let's face it is he worth it? Waltz of banknotes and nothing is good enough.

Blinded by love. What a poor, silly girl, she's swallowing everything. I don't even know if I'm going to be used so, superstitiously, she puts me in the closet. I'm waiting ...

Why has she encumbered herself with an object of my size? She's not straight in the head. Only three short days. Eh! Wake up sleeping beauty who waits for the kiss of prince charming! All the same, what a pity! I have the feeling that I'm going to be very heavy, but at this time she's the one who's being very heavy.

Note, in French all big traveling luggage is feminine. One wonders why. Lets get on with it. *La* suitcase, even better, *la* trunk, even *la* vanity case (hypocritical) but *le* handbag, *le* briefcase (yuck again an anglicism). In short, I'm getting lost — not at the airport I hope, that would be the last straw. Me, an object of added value, am getting lost in my simple thoughts in order to forget how much she irritates me. And she looks and looks at me again and again. We have to say that as an object, a suitcase can be quite admirable. . . . Oh well if I had a bit of gumption, unlike her sorry to say, I would say that she is looking at me, more than that, that she is contemplating me, for my concept.

Oh! Am I dreaming or what? Three weeks before the trip and, bang, just like that, I jumped out of the closet. And one dress, two dresses, five dresses. How I pity her. She's completely cracked. Is she going to change every half hour or what? I actually have extra space. I hope she's not going to use it all. I'm relieved not having a brain if it is for using this way. And I'm not even speaking about sex. I already have a gender and my own style. It is enough.

She fills me up and empties me over and over. From an utilitarian object, I'm becoming the object of all her focus. Take care, here come the lingerie. Not bad. I hope that at least he will appreciate that. I'm cracking up. I'm sure I'm going to stay in the closet. She's really not very cunning, this little weasel. And I have the IQ of a suitcase.

Oh well, what I was saying. She just tossed me into the very bottom of the closet one week before the trip. I won't describe to you the mood. No. She's just a fatalistic femme fatale. Deep in herself she knew, but she wanted to try her luck anyway. Yet, filled in haste and without enthusiasm this time, I made a trip.

How stubborn she is, this one, when she really wants something.

"Unforgettable, unforgettable," he said. I hope this happens for her. She deserves it after all the effort she puts into him. In the meantime, given all she's put into me, I weigh close to 50 pounds and she has to carry me. She's crazy.

LINGUISTICS AND PROSE
FOURTH PAUSE

I have a passion for languages, fascinated by the fact that humans, although having identical physiology, invented so many different codes of communication. So many ways to understand or not to understand each other.

So I have always been attracted to the foreign and to strangers. Stranger is a strange word, revealing clearly our apprehensive approach to what doesn't look like us, or, I come back to this idea, what we don't understand.

The stranger it is the more it talks to me and tells me to want to understand. Another way of life, another culture, another way to see and name things.

Each language contains the culture. To possess a language is therefore to possess the keys that provide access to cultural identity. It is interesting to note that in Chinese the word "spouse" is written — since one of the ways this language functions is picto-ideographically — "broom" + "belly" and that the term has never changed. But when the Chinese had to create a new word for "computer", they had to concretize the concept and came up with "brain" + "electricity". This demonstrates that we have to add a modern touch to follow the evolution of society, but not for a "spouse" apparently. Similarly, the word "peace" is written with a "woman" under a "roof", while the word "dispute" is portrayed by "three women" under "one roof". Sometimes two are enough . . .

I chose some of my lovers because they came from other countries and thus spoke a different language. This filled a need in me to satisfy my curiosity about the other. Also, I like that my lovers speak to me in a language other than mine, as I have been bilingual, even trilingual since birth. It arouses me greatly when a man whispers in my ear words I do not always understand when I make love.

And he chose English to converse with me …

I liked it immediately. Unique, erotic, exotic experience.

I learned during my studies, and also empirically, that when one has a strong emotion it can only be expressed in the mother tongue. And as a philosopher or writer, whose name I forgot, said, "We can only express love in our mother tongue." I agree with this idea, because love is an emotion.

But he spoke of love and sex in a language other than that of his birth language. Although I found this beautiful and extremely well expressed in terms of semantics and syntax, the impact I felt on reading him was very different when he was expressing himself in French.

But the aspect of playfulness is not to be ignored. We shared a game, a joust, very sexually electrifying and exhilarating, in which one could perceive the conversation rising to reach the sacred and the consecrated — the ultimate revelation of the body and, secondarily, of the heart and the soul.

I wondered about the use of English. It was a game, a role, which kept everything unreal. The real cannot admit the seriousness or the evidence of the feeling experienced. It was a form of acting. Everything was acceptable, since the role will expire at the end of the play and everyone will take back his identity — identity constructed by the natural use of the native language.

I was at this moment of my analytical thoughts when ...

From: **FB**
To: **Liz**

Strange, among so many other strange features: I only write to you in English, whereas we speak French when we talk. Do you mind? Some words sound nicer in French than in English, some the other way round. For the first time, I write down that I'm focused on your *gorge*, your *lèvres*, your *chatte*, your *allure* ... With you.

From: **FB**
To: **Liz**

Tu es exquise (So there, I wrote to you in French!)

From: **FB**
To: **Liz**

You speak English, I answer in French. Do I deserve the type of love you think of for me? No French, unconsciously.

From: **FB**
To: **Liz**

I'm hastening to read you! In English or in French? I hesitate also regarding the tongue (!) that you are expecting from me in this exercise. Just tell me.

Subtle blend of the two languages and the two tongues. He whispered that to me ...

Had he read my mind? I adored when he was writing me in English for the reasons I mentioned before, but, strangely, when I was reading him in French it was not him anymore. I told him this feeling and, gently, he came back to the English. But after a huge problem in his life, he wrote me essentially in French. He surprised himself —"Here I am writing in French!"

An indisputable fact that I witnessed repeatedly in my work with foreigners is that true emotion can only be expressed in the mother tongue. Consequently, his messages expressed in French found a direct path to my heart. The word "heart" seems to me too romantic, too limited, but I cannot find another one. It made the thing more serious in my eyes. Somewhere, he gave up playing a role and entered the ground floor of reality. The need for reassurance led to the use of our common language. Or was it an evolution of the relationship? I never found the answer. It never occurred to us to express ourselves verbally in a language other than French.

About Conflict
Fifth Panel

Every human relationship, and, more extensively, any relationship between living things, goes through conflict. The development and formation of the human personality in the child, and also in that of baby animals, passes through opposition in which we take the measure of the other. To rub up against the other sets limits and determines the lines which are not to be crossed. One triumphs, the other dies or surrenders. It is a question of domination or submission and of affirming who we are.

The balance of power is dictated by existence itself. The notion of survival is based on supremacy. Fortunately, evolution has civilized this concept but it is revealed every day in a subtle and watered down way. However, it is always showing its essence as it is inherent in biology and, so, inevitable.

One major difference between people is the art of managing this inevitable conflict. When poorly managed, it can escalate into war — literally and figuratively. The extreme expression of non-resolution of conflict is murder, murder of passion or murder of war (literal murders) and, more subtly, a continual abrasiveness to the point where the essence of the other disappears (figurative murder).

Of course our relationship, although virtual because it only existed through the written word — no raising of voices, shrugging of shoulders, rolling of eyes — did not escape this form of exaggerated communication. Everything came to a head one day after one of his emails got lost in the vast digestive machinery of the printed circuit boards of computers, machinery not understood and hence magical for me.

Perhaps a trivial occurrence, but it was a letter of key importance for the development and the continuity of our relationship in order to bring us to the next level.

As I mentioned before, I don't trust anyone now, and any 'bug' causes me mistrust and suspicion, having in the back of my mind the concept of two ways of being betrayed. Betrayal by lying, which is its most elementary form. Or betrayal by an adverse and harmful action, which is its most elaborate form.

He wrote then . . .

From: **FB**
To: **Liz**

This Sunday. Intense panic: do you receive my letters (three burning letters in 24 hours)? I fear a computer malfunction. Reassure me, if necessary.

From: **FB**
To: **Liz**

Please answer me about your receiving of this mail, which I'm sending thru another way.

From: **FB**
To: **Liz**

I don't know what to do. My emails have not reached you. I'm desperate. I know nothing about technology. I'll try to call you tomorrow, Monday morning, without waking you up: shooting. I had written you one of my most beautiful letters . . .

To which I replied . . .

From: **Liz**
To: **FB**

F. You find your letters or it is me that you will never found again.

The intensity of my emotion due to my anger made me make a basic grammar error! In retrospect, I think his writings still contained a grain of truth. I didn't care about his truth, the friction was there, he would not step on my limits. No one frustrates me that way. You don't pass a cake under my nose and say, "Too bad. It was the best cake I ever made for you. Na na na . . ."

He wrote back . . .

From: **FB**
To: **Liz**

No threats, please!

By the tenor of his answer, I think he perceived the gravity of the situation and my seriousness. I usually do not say anything unless I really mean it and he knew it. When he did send me a summary of the contents of "his most beautiful letters", which I did indeed find very beautiful, it calmed me down and the situation returned to normal.

Evidently he was not mastering technological communication via the computer. But my assumptions were that he actually was experiencing a certain modesty towards me. This excessive consideration could be the source of a fib and an attempt to prepare the ground for his future, more sexual emails. Assuming he was right about the fact that he had never written that way to any woman, perhaps he felt some fear as to how I would respond to letters so blue. A rejection from me was still possible. He had already experienced my impulsiveness and bluntness.

But I cannot believe he had never written that way to anyone. What was I to think of him, how could I perceive him after receiving such hot confessions in such an expressive vocabulary. Without any doubt this could prove to be a problem. One must proceed slowly on shifting sands.

It was obvious that since the first look at each other we both knew what we wanted and what would be the outcome. But the process beyond the end-in-itself is interesting and plays like a chess game. He moved his queen, but he better watch out for my knight. Nothing should be left unguarded, or you'll loose the game. But there is nothing less tangible than a relationship orchestrated through computers. So he was psychologically preparing me for these more daring future emails, sharpening my curiosity with finesse.

This was my first assumption based on the fact that the technology of sending and storing emails is a very reliable one. Men, subjected to excessive pressures that sometimes can stifle them, often find a safety valve in lying. Some men master this art to perfection and, although it is not their original intention, are driven by the trap that can close behind them at any time. I understand it perfectly, even though I have a devoted hatred of lies. Not to address the truth, or to hide it by omission, although more hypocritical, suits me better anyway.

The second assumption was that he was telling the truth, but it would surprise me if he really was. Hence my wrath.

Hunting is not always easy for these poor representatives of the male species. I understand and sympathize. A man functions physiologically as follows — for the survival of the species he must mate as much as possible and spread his seed everywhere to protect life. That's why I don't believe in the notion of being coupled for life. And, in fact, I pity the male species who must juggle these two factors — the uncontrollable desire that engenders procreation and the social morality that directs the family cell. Then, on top of it, when love, with its exclusive contract gets mixed in, life becomes chaotic.

I came to this level of compassion and indulgence towards men recently, just after the death of my father. His life has been without any doubt one of the most chaotic. He had a lot of women. He was awesome and very charming. He had many children with many different women. Although he abandoned me, I've always devoted a great love to him.

When I inquired of him in order to find out why he had so many children whom he didn't take care of, at least the first ones and the last ones, he had this answer which I didn't expect, "In order not to die."

When he did die, I received absolutely no expression of sympathy from anyone. Nobody forgave him about how he led his life. Then I began to reflect heavily on that inflexible lack of compassion even in the face of death and I tried to understand it. Hence this analysis of the male condition.

PARENTHETICAL CHAPTER
TO SYNTHESIZE

Having arrived at this point in my story, it is my heartfelt desire to precisely express that all the ideas and analyses I'm enunciating regarding these different metaphysical approaches involve only and absolutely only me. Because of a lack of mentors, since childhood I've learned how to think and reflect on my own. And, as I've already explained, I was resistant to all forms of book learning, even though I've always found books to be a source of great pleasure and an excellent way to become self-taught. However, I'm made in such a way that even made wealthy and enriched by this empirical knowledge and distilled experience of others, I have my own way of thinking about my environment. I also have a very critical mind which perceives all the details like a child, because I remained a child who never had enough of my parents.

So all my ideas that I've been talking about are dictated by personal experience followed by analysis. I do this in order not to suffer anymore, to evolve, and to forge my personality without guidance and that way become enriched. It seems to me that one can be more creative and more efficient when one's mind is not constrained by prior learning. I have proof of this in my recent film experience. To be in the role of a novice actress was easy because I am innocent. I want to say that I was not restrained by the shackles of learning and, consequently, was able to unleash my emotions, and make my expressions closer to my reality and myself, not influenced at all by education. I was told that this reflected on the screen to great effect.

In the next chapters I will discuss other basic topics that paved the way of my life. I reiterate the fact that my approach to reasoning may not be truly revolutionary and may not be completely off the beaten path. I do not have this pretension. So, from my own experiences, I get my own morality which I'm transmitting with this marvelous computer object, that I tame a little better each day, and which is related to my brain with its many twists and turns.

ON JEALOUSY
SIXTH PART

From: FB
To: Liz

You know what? I'm afraid I'd be awfully jealous if someone even touched your skin! I am certain of the uniqueness of our relationship, in words, in thoughts, in sex attraction. I easily admit other men's desperate courting, it sounds just normal to me. You are so breath-taking. I think of you constantly, with devotion, expectation, desire, tenderness. I am not so far away, please keep it in your European, romantic, different mind. I'm yours, all.

From: FB
To: Liz

Thanks for the precious gift: not so many can claim they know your phone numbers, isn't it? Be sure I'll make a quite selective use of them. I felt your looking at me while on stage one hour ago, it was ever so sweet and exciting. At a time you crossed your legs for me, I could hardly remain concentrated. I see you in black because of those stills. Except this scarlet lipstick of yours! Be sure I call you soon. Be sure you haunt my dreams. Be sure [...] is not so far away from [...]. Yours.

He later confided to me that every time he called me — very often during the night because of the difference in time zones, certainly, but perhaps also subconsciously to make sure that no other man was sharing my nights — as soon as he was dialing my number he developed the most remarkable erection, very embarrassing because difficult to hide. For who else could I have crossed my legs?

[. . .] proved to be far away from [. . .]

From: **FB**
To: **Liz**

Another point. Strangely, I am jealous of this outstanding Russian guy, who obviously looked nicer than I do, and pleased you intensely at first sight. I am afraid your next chapter will deal with your sex complicity. Now, I claim that no one ever conceived for you those thoughts I let you know about. And I want to be sure you never wrote to anybody the kind of literature you send me.

Forgive the over simplicity of those feelings: I feel awkward, but unable not to confess it all. We agreed on our mutual total frankness.

Your red lips, your black lashes, your glorious tits, your wonderful arse are meant for me, as well as your art of love. I hope you never mentioned your tongue before: the crazy making games you play with it are privately owned...

This Russian guy he spoke of was one of my lovers. In one of my books in which I am sharing all my love affairs, this Russian lover holds a prominent place in my story for some of his characteristics, including his exceptional beauty and the uncommon color of his eyes. Also he revealed to me some skills of love I did not know. So, yes, his jealousy was justified when he wrote, but one cannot be jealous of a memory and he greatly appreciated my ability to love by this lover revealed.

From: **FB**
To: **Liz**

Some sort of a love dream, spiritual and sensual. We shall proceed, further and deeper. I can almost feel the taste of your intimate liquor flowing into my throat while I kiss and lick your erected love mount. And can hardly wait till you make my cock yours, exclusively.

I didn't expect it. He was experiencing feelings of jealousy unfortunately closely linked to love, which left me puzzled and perplexed. Following the lead of Marcel Proust, we approach the problem backwards. For him, it is jealousy that engenders love. The lack of a person or worry that she's looking somewhere else, makes her more present and ever more haunting. This is Proust's principle of love. Whatever the real theory, I couldn't believe that he loved me and, above all, I didn't want to believe it. Our love story in real life was destined for a dead end. An impasse on one hand, punctuated by "when and where" for our meetings. To join him occasionally at one of his professional gatherings across the country seemed in the realm of possibility, but could not be done on a regular basis due to many reasons that both he and I were aware of. I was wondering if his schedule allowed him the slightest possibility of flexibility-freedom to join me? And, beyond everything, did he really want to? I didn't feel that he did.

Impasse on the other hand regarding the nature of my status inherent in the position he wanted and/or could offer me in his life. It was a chaotic relationship very difficult to maintain from a material point of view and in a space-time continuum. That left emails, perhaps tiring, redundant and meaningless in the long run, since malnourished. The topic of actually getting together was very delicate and so, of course, absolutely never mentioned. So we will be in love only for the beauty, emotion, vibration and memories without ever anchoring it in reality, only dream time via electronic epistles. This was the only plausible explanation because, to take form in reality, the wings given by love would have to move mountains. Could this love rise to the challenge? My rational mind knows the answer, but I have to accommodate myself to the concept of love that is populating my thoughts. I too am a dreamer.

All of these statements, when analyzed, dissected, enunciated, however, do not necessarily raise doubts about his sincerity. Unfortunately, I am absolutely unable to have sexual relations with a man without any feeling because, without feeling mixed with sexuality, my life would have been much simpler but also less intense. But everything is only a question of balance. The differences lie in the intensity and depth of feeling experienced that I could grade as follows: devouring consuming passion; passion; crazy love; love; crush; tenderness. Looking closely at my list, the word that attracted me the most is "love" because, in its simplicity, it reveals the essential. I didn't want to feel too much love for him. I wanted him to be in the diminuendo of my list. Yet, but, if something in the world exists that is so irrational and uncontrollable as the attraction for the other, I would like to know what. In brief, will and volition have no voice in this chapter. Love has this imperative side. It imposes itself without asking the opinion of its victim and acts in conquered territory. It sticks to the skin like a tattoo.

I knew he was engaged and so untouchable.

So why was he playing the love card? To push the game to its extreme? To have the leisure to dream? Or the better to make me succumb? To be sure of achieving the goal by this thorny path? He knew that there would be only three days of sharing. He had planned it so. Then I knew it also.

My way of being, very down to earth and very close to the conceivable and the real, tells me not to venture on this path.

To take this adventure like a candy that melts in the mouth and disappears in the stomach after three minutes of pleasure experienced on the tongue. In this case it was three days.

I also knew empirically that men claim exclusivity of their conquest with or without feelings. It is very difficult for me to comment on this. I've always noticed that, although intuition is classed as a predominantly female characteristic, men experience it perfectly when their capture escapes them.

I have experienced situations worthy of vaudeville. One of the most *rocambolesque* went like this: I had a new lover for the first time in my bed, a previous lover knocking on my door and an antepenultimate on the phone at 10:00 o'clock on a Sunday morning. Of course I had already broken up with the two previous lovers. I have to say this just in case . . . Needless to describe my embarrassment! I dealt with it not too badly because of my prompt wit and spirit and an ability to handle unexpected circumstances.

Similarly, perhaps he will remember it because he was looking at me at that time. The night I met him I received a very unusual text message from my current lover. We were essentially communicating by email so this text was surprising and unexpected. Had he sensed what was going on? Happenstance always challenge me. Remember, we use only 5% of our brain capacity. Some of us use perhaps a bit more.

My husband called me one evening to ask me how I was doing while I was at a restaurant with a man who would become my lover. Since the beginning of our marriage, I basically led a single life style and often went out by myself. Not by choice, but because my husband imposed it on me by never wanting to go out with me. Never before was he concerned about me having a good time when I was out by myself. But I must say that it was the first time I was actually with another man whom I liked and who became my lover that night.

I have many other examples which brought me to the conclusion that men perceive when "their" woman will soon no longer be theirs. And this sense of ownership seems very strange to me. I recently had a conversation with a friend who told me that jealousy and love are inseparable. The obligations of love imply exclusivity. Jealousy is provoked by a sense of remoteness in the other and the threat that they will develop an attraction for someone else. Though, if there is any attraction for someone else, it is because love or desire for the original lover has faded or worse. Most men and many women do not need love to make love. Everything is simple then. Could he afford to continue to court me so provocatively and still ignore real feeling? It was cavalier, but certainly real. Maybe too much. And, as I wrote earlier, men claim exclusivity for their conquest even without feeling love, just by instinct.

About love, with him I was really torn between the desire to believe in it and the need not to believe in it. One was feeding my dreamy sky, the other my realistic earth land. Between heaven and earth, I still have not decided. I do not want to decide. Even if . . .

Jealousy in my opinion is related to feelings of insecurity and lack of confidence. But this is a basic and poor explanation. Too simplistic for what can be concealed by this complex feeling which is mixed at the same time with dignity and something less dignified. I've always known men to be jealous, very jealous. But their way of expressing it was often very different. Another of my writings focuses on these emotions of life.

I have been obviously confronted with this feeling of jealousy myself, but my first thought was to try to understand why the man whom I was extremely in love with had to get away from me and go to another woman. I must have opened a door. I needed to understand in order to find a remedy and not to keep making the same mistake. I have always preferred to break everything and start over elsewhere rather than live with a man for whom I didn't count as before. Because, when you glue the teapot, it is less pretty and, on top of everything, it leaks. I needed a lot of strength to do this, but I wanted to choose my road. This experience gave me the strength to better realize the next love. The love life is made to surround the beloved all the time that love lasts. But I think everything dies, even love. And we also acknowledge that love and passion, after a while, develop into lassitude. So languid love to eat for enthusiasts who demand it, eager for all the vortex of emotions that make us feel so beautiful and so alive and makes us consecrate the pleasure as the absolute. How to keep this emotion muted when it is so deep and loud within us? Because this is not really us. He and I are made from the same wood. We are passionate lovers of passion. To be, then, intelligent and imaginative enough to make this passion live long without any injuries. I am dreaming of that. Until now the only one I could feel who had this unusual capacity was him. I only had him in my life for five months of sharing words and three days of sharing love. Above all, not to make Mallarmé a liar — a beautiful story for a beautiful book.

I adored his strong and more than romantic texts that literally transported me and I was touched by his need to be unique for me. He was. He made me discover moments of life that overwhelmed me with emotion. A rare ability that I never experienced in this way before.

FROM THE VIRTUAL TO THE REAL
SEXUAL CRESCENDO
SEVENTH HEAVEN

1 HE

I do declare that never had any man written to me the way he did regarding the quality and quantity. One of my deepest dreams was always to fuse those words concerning lovemaking. Did his writing prefigure his ultimate sexual excellence? Everything suggested it. The computer exchange created an extremely exciting sense of anticipation. It was feeding all the fantasies and all the expectations. Each of his texts was extremely voluptuous and moving. I read them over and over again with increasing desire. The fact that since the very beginning of our correspondence, he perceived me always very precisely never ceased to amaze me. I couldn't help thinking, while I strongly restrained myself, that we were made for each other and that, without a doubt, our mutual understanding would be intellectual, sensual and sexual.

I did not know at this time that our sexual concepts initiated on a piece of paper, or rather on the screen, would take place in reality. We respected all that was drafted. Like an architect's plan that turns into a house.

EROTIC SCENE ONE ...

VIRTUALITY ...

From: **FB**
To: **Liz**

But the wonderful tips of your breasts are exposed as never before! Thank you for offering them in their soft pink and bright volume, although they are not (yet) stiffened with pleasure. Red and black are the colors of your sexiest lingerie. I take everything you give to me and I become satiated. It enchants me. Kisses, yes, and much more.

REALITY ...

The tips of my breasts he saw for the first time in my bath water. He had this following request. "May I attend?" A doubt in me. "Attend?" To my diving into the hot tub? Attend to what, in fact? Reflecting later on, I think that indeed it was this intimate bathing scene that he wanted to attend. But he was so made that perceiving a very slight hesitation, suggesting resistance from the other person, would make him retreat. My expressive eyes made him understand that he was being a little too inquisitive for an initial approach.

So, because I had to empty my suitcase, he let me understand that it was this unpacking he wanted to share with me. He was looking at me putting out all I had carefully prepared for him, to please him, to shine for him, and, by extension, for us. To adorn myself for love ...

I found him very sweet in his voice, in his gestures, in his words, in his attentions. But my feelings were mixed. I felt at the same time like a little girl who was showing all her toys to the person she loved, and kind of like a call girl. The word "call girl" is too strong and somewhat inappropriate, but I never before joined a man I didn't know in reality in an hotel bedroom to make love. But it is wrong to say that I didn't know him after all these months of email exchanges.

At the same time I was very confident and comfortable around him, chatting with him in a pleasant and natural way while I was unpacking my suitcase. I felt the need to refresh myself. Plane trips are not really conducive to feeling beautiful and desirable.

I couldn't resist the bathtub. I always found bathtubs too small for my long legs, but I love to languish in the tub. He ran the water for me. It had been a long time since I had such masculine attention, and I didn't know how to react in front of such eagerness.

Pleasure of the hot water on my skin. Pleasure to be naked. Pleasure and temptation to feel him so close. I was in the water and I was about to dive in deeper. I called him. Usually I'm a modest person and I don't like to show myself naked. But with him I felt no shyness. Kneeling beside the tub, the sleeves of his jacket soaking in the water, he began to caress and gaze at me. First he took my breasts in his mouth and the peaks "were stiffened with pleasure".

I loved the silky soft touch. My most exciting recollection remains when he looked at my sex and began to stroke and open it. I still have the expression of his capsized eyes in my memory. Soft voluptuousness. Then he asked me to make him taste my love-juice. "Put a finger in your pussy and give it to me" and I did so shamelessly with the desire to please him. I can still see my middle finger engulfed between his lips. And he took everything I gave him. I was ready to fulfill his every whim. I leave to him to express if he was "satiated" and "enchanted". Regarding the "kisses" we exchanged a lot of, I found his tongue very soft and the "much more" arrived . . .

EROTIC SCENE TWO . . .

VIRTUALITY . . .

From: FB
To: Liz

There is one essence you did not mention, ever so crucial, which exudes from our mouths when we kiss, which will shine upon your lips and mine, crown your nipples and fill up your sex, cover up my cock till the long awaited moment when all our intimate liquors taste and exhale the same. I will spend this coming day thinking of this special fusion. A special day, then. Yours, yours.

REALITY . . .

The only secretions that the human body exudes and that are for me not only tolerable but are also appreciated, are tears, sperm and feminine liquor. Not only for their emotional connotation but also because of my taste for their tastes. I shared this peculiarity with him and I do declare that what he said about the mixture of the water of our mouths distilled in the most intimate parts of our body, caressed my skin, my heart, and my soul. What I saw as unique and specific, he made plural, like the possessive adjective "our" he used to describe the hotel room that made the experience equal and as shared as our secretions. He handled the duo with brio. This aptitude, this ability, made him to me admirable and precious. Our mouths united and mingled their water over and over again and he said to me, "The kiss is an act of love, strong and voluptuous, quite comparable to sexual union, don't you think?" I had in my mouth all our interwoven flavors and never told him that the taste of his sperm was my favorite liquor.

VIRTUALITY . . .

From: **FB**
To: **Liz**

How big they are. How beautiful they are. How erect they are. How much pleasure they should bring you. I will suck them. I will bite them until they become huge and make you come like you like. I imagine them already stiff springing from your bra, soon stretched and made shiny by my kisses, filling my mouth with their hugeness. O, how I wish to celebrate your breasts and make you proud of them! Imagine the crazy pleasure that you will offer me when they envelope my disproportionate sex and the throbbing point of my cock strokes your nipples, and then your greedy lips will have their turn to suck! I fuck you, and much more if there is an affinity . . .

REALITY . . .

The future tense — "I will suck them, I will bite them" — became the present tense. Present also his erect sex. The first time in general is not always exceptional. We have to discover each other and uncover our eroticism. With him it was fluid. But there was still in me a restraint and also I didn't understand why I had thoughts about my previous lover. The brain is really extremely complex.

The only thing that surprised me was his eyes. I realized later that his desire made them appear watery and troubled. He "fucked me" and "affinity" arose later when our bodies became more acquainted.

EROTIC SCENE THREE . . .

VIRTUALITY . . .

From: FB
To: Liz

With such happiness! Yes. I fuck you. I fill you with me. I nourish myself from you and you fall asleep fulfilled by pleasure. I only saw you furtively in reality and with your clothes on. Now I have feasted on your photo, half naked and adorned for love. I am waiting for you. Soon, you will be dressed for me. Little by little your clothes will fade away — a striptease with four hands. We will be one to the other and one in the other. The expression of your look, even if exhausted, speaks your tender emotion. I fuck your depths, Liz. You are coming without stopping. My come springs up to your heart.

REALITY . . .

I dressed for him and he undressed me like he wanted. Initially half, and then completely. He took off my love attire. We were "one to another, one in the other" and, yes, "my eyes were exhausted and excited". When he penetrated me this time my pleasure was extreme, my desire at its pinnacle. I was feeling him perfectly in me and I was only this burning pussy of which he had spoken. His words amplified my pleasure because of their sensuality and evocativeness. I like it that he would comment on what he was seeing and what he was feeling in a very direct, raw and tender way. I was also expecting the unexpected. I wanted him to take me as I had never been taken before — at the same time with softness and violence. And he did it. I recall the sound of the rustling of the sheets when his body changed positions, noise that made me wait for what was to follow and made me wait for what was to come. I wanted that these moments would last for hours and that his hard manhood would caress me inside and fulfill me in both senses of the term.

EROTIC SCENE FOUR ...

VIRTUALITY ...

From: **FB**
To: **Liz**

Right now you are sleeping, you are dreaming of love, you are aroused, your nightgown is soaked, as are your panties and g-string, as during the day when you think of me. How they move me, damp and heavy with your intimate secretions, whose abundance, flavor and fragrance drive me crazy! I kiss them with full mouth and through them your intimacy is torn open with desire. I always knew your taste for sexy lingerie, reveling impertinently in your bait — I like that word. Very *Grand Siècle* — and I wonder when you conceived this red and black photo gallery. Regarding your intimate wardrobe, you just added the most exquisite detail — the black gloves of love. I am dreaming to see you wear them at our next meeting. I know that you will have some ideas about the most exciting use you can make of them. Sex, passion, tenderness. It will be delicious. I feel right now that I am only my cock, enormous, raw, painful, waiting for you. I know that you will give it the most unforgettable attention.

REALITY ...

In fact, he kissed and licked the intimate secrets of my underwear, making sure not to loose any drop of this precious liquid. I would have liked that everything of me would be as precious. I knew to give to his manhood the most unforgettable attention, bringing to it all my tenderness, gentleness and passion. Tenderness of my tongue on the skin of his engorged sex, filled with desire for me. Passion in my eyes darted to his. Tenderness of my gloved hands that gently stroked his cock, passion of my nails on his flesh sacks filled with sperm that he said he would save for me so I could cause it to spring forth whenever I would like.

VIRTUALITY . . .

From: **FB**
To: **Liz**

Exactly what I'm dreaming of. You know the secret of men. You guessed mine. This gesture, "so commonplace and so represented", you accomplish it being an expert of beauty and intuition. You're wrong, it's extremely rare. You, you know what the expectations of a man's penis are. I want to wear the lipsticked impression of your mouth on my cock and hear comments in my ear about the gestures of love that fulfill you as well as me. My cum boiling in my balls is tense and painful, it is yours.

REALITY . . .

By nature I am very applied and very much a perfectionist and whatever I do I want the fruits of my labors to satisfy me. To waste time and energy for a lower result does not please me. So when it comes to giving pleasure to a man close to my heart I devote myself fully.

He spoke to me of the fear experienced by some women facing a man's sex, a concept totally strange to me. I never even thought about it. For me a man's sex is a source of pleasure . . . for two. I love everything — the shape, smoothness, firmness, taste, slip, small creases and folds. So I did not have enough of my mouth, my lips, my tongue and my teeth to suck it, stroke it, lick it, and caress it. While my eyes were planted in his, I was applying myself to distill the pleasure I could see growing in his eyes. I felt like making him come.

I love to watch.

All knowledge is power, all pleasure is addiction. I know and I can provide this type of caress for hours, always with the same enthusiasm. My hands know the rhythm and also how to get lost where they are appreciated.

VIRTUALITY . . .

From: **FB**
To: **Liz**

I want your so expert lips open on my sex, as your tongue caresses the most sensitive part of my cock, that your hands jerk it with love and that your long lacquered nails travel the length and tension of its shaft. When the cum wells forth you will drink the first sips with relish, the following ones will flood your face, your belly and your breasts. Do you approve of this wonderful program of love — among many others to describe and to live?

REALITY . . .

My carmine red and brilliant lips were opened on his cock, my tongue caressed the most sensitive parts of his shaft, my hands have wanked with love and my nails have traveled its length and tension. I approved this wonderful program.

VIRTUALITY...

From: **FB**
To: **Liz**

I will flood you with my sperm, your favorite liquor. I'd like to seduce you with my cock and my cum. Its flavor, scent, consistency will delight you. As I'm writing, my erection is violent and painful! But my cock stroked, sucked, wanked by you will get twice as big. You will love it.

REALITY...

His cock was stroked, sucked and wanked by me. It gets twice as big. I loved it. Everything seduced me.

VIRTUALITY...

From: **FB**
To: **Liz**

O, those love gloves on your wrists, Liz, that you wear to stroke my cock, of course. You write me of love and desire and in the middle of the night we almost faint.

REALITY...

I wore my love gloves to stroke his cock. I spoke to him about love and desire, and we fainted with pleasure in the middle of the night.

FINALLY, VIRTUAL REALITY . . .

From: **FB**
To: **Liz**

With such an emotion! Softly, slowly, at the very beginning, my cock will penetrate your cunt exhausted with kisses and caresses, that you will open for me with your beautiful, painted nails. I enter you with the width and breath and my dick, so raw because you have sucked and wanked it a lot. In the depths of your being, my penis touches the end as it reaches your heart. So I fuck you with violence. I make you scream with pleasure. We almost lose consciousness because of our intense desire for each other. You come without stopping, taking my sex between the lips of your pussy, sticky with come as your mouth was before. I'm going to come in your depths. When finally the sperm bursts forth, we think we are dying of ecstasy.

I have nothing to add. It all happened exactly as he stated a month before . . .

2 SHE

She also went briskly from the virtual text to the real action, erasing that way any frustration she had experienced before.

From: **Liz**
To: **FB**

F. If you only could see my breasts. At this moment of my cycle, they are at maximum fullness. Although they are a bit painful, I count on you to stroke them and kiss them, to take the tips between your teeth, to turn this pain into an intense pleasure. It is one of my favorite erogenous zones. You know it.
I want your crazy kisses in the pit of my neck to make me shudder. I want your hands to caress the inside of my thighs before diving into my privacy. I want you make me come before — it boosts my pleasure — and I want you to penetrate me so softly, following the cadence and rhythm that I will give you thanks to my flexible back. I want your crazy kisses on my tongue and your sweet and crazy words.

I was horribly missing his eyes, his gaze fixed on me, on my body. I was feeling beautiful and desirable thanks to and because of him and I wanted him to see it in order to realize it. The frustration I felt gave rise to all these elaborate descriptions I created because of his physical absence. I add this qualifier "physical" to the word "absence" because in my heart and in my soul he was more than present. Then I unleashed all my fantasies, my awake dreams, as if giving them birth with my thoughts. I expressed with words what I will share with him to cool down my intense frustration. He took care with attention and delicacy all the parts mentioned above and he made me love low tide and high tide.

My Words . . .

From: Liz
To: FB

Chapter One: Fiction
We have a meeting at a hotel room at the seaside.
I'm waiting for you. I'm in a hot, perfumed bath and I feel lascivious and airy tasting the tranquility of the place and smelling the beneficial water foaming in the tub. I prepare my body for you. It will be soft, fragrant and inviting. I tame my hair, apply my makeup carefully as you like. I splash myself with two perfumes because I like to be unique, and I wrap myself in a Rita Hayworthian bathrobe. I strap my body in a black corset, a thong, and nylons laced high to where the garters attach. I check to see if I am beautiful enough.
When finally you arrive, I will be tantalizing, moistening my lips with my tongue, surreptitiously caressing the tops of my breasts with my fine painted fingers. Or, alternately, adjusting my straps and my garters. And I will paint my mouth voluptuously with cherry lip gloss, sliding my lips on each other in anticipation of a kiss. I bring desire to its paroxysmal state. Only the look, that's all I allowed you to do. Since we are sipping a little alcohol to disinhibit us this first time, alcohol that you can lick from my lips when, after penetrating looks and penetrating words, we develop intense desire for each other and become unable to wait any longer. I would like then that, with tenderness and boldness, you ravish me on the bed, cover me with kisses and bites, all with an incomparable softness. And now takes place your love scene.

In response to his love scene . . .

From: Liz
To: FB

I didn't continue your narrative. I just wrote its preface, because preliminaries are a feminine instinct, my love.
Carmine red lips shining with gloss, long nails of the same red, eyes surrounded with black, eyelashes long and thickened with mascara, wild hair scattered on the pillow. Body-coated and milk flavored with sweet and heady gardenia, a leotard and shoes with killer sharp heels and blood-red silk robe. She is lying voluptuously, half opens her robe, her thighs revealing a thin string concealing the center of her sex. Since the leotard is indented between her thighs, she has easy access and slides a finger under the strap to release her flesh and intimately caresses it with dexterity and softness. She pushes a finger into her vagina, allowing herself to sense both the sweetness of the interior dampness on her finger and the movement of her finger in her sex. She bites her lips . . .

The meal I created for him . . .

From: Liz
To: FB

As an aperitif and appetizer I offer you a bit of strip-tease with Liz sauce — I've never done it before. I swear and promise you. But, I don't know why, it seems to me that you will love it.
Imagine my hands sliding over my thighs to reveal the flesh, removing my leotard. Imagine the lace and string that I will very gently slide between my legs, stroking myself. Imagine my imprisoned breasts so happy to finally feel free, trembling because of the softness of my hands waiting for you to admire the erect nipples. Imagine my coal-voluptuous eyes clouded with desire for you. Imagine my mouth shiny because moistened by my tongue. Imagine my naked body, heads and tails unveiled just for your eyes.

As a first course: my most volatile and subtle caresses all over your body. Imagine my eyelashes on your cheek and on your neck, on your belly and your sex. Imagine my kisses, my caresses on your lips and all over. I have the urge just to make you shiver, pant and become erect.

As a main course: my mouth, my lips and my tongue gently busying themselves to give the most extreme pleasure to the most sensitive part of you. I'll make you cum in my mouth? . . . Maybe . . .

For desert: My sex offered to your gaze, to your hands, to your lips, to your cock, which penetrating me will provoke the most sucked, blown and sensual sighs and groans.

For alcohol: Our arpeggio-orgasm intoxicated with passion and vintage, our voice-whispers exchanging Armagnac-words and liqueur-phrases.

As a digestive: Eau de vie will end our feast with splendor.

Since I wanted him to devour me so much, I composed this meal of love just for him. He also often spoke of his love for me using graphic terms of ingestion and digestion: "I'm drinking you; I'm drinking your mouth; I'm hungry and thirsty for you; I am nourishing myself from you." The physical, our mouths, mingling with the metaphysical, the one nourishing the other, revealing the most extreme love of all.

As he had always announced, predicted, anticipated, visualized, and extrapolated, we fed off each other. He was like a director who honed his script before filming. He transcended me.

From: **Liz**
To: **FB**

I open my crimson-dressed mouth as your cock darts toward me. I welcome it in between my lips so you can feel the softness, wetness and pressure. Close your eyes and feel me. My hand, at once delicate and strong, grips your cock and proceeds with a move that harmonizes with the suction of my mouth. My tongue is having a very slow walk and shamelessly infiltrates everything you want to offer to me and everything I'm taking from you. My eyes, dressed in black, planted in yours, express the drowning of the light in the troubled waters of desire. You can see my breasts would like to be stroked and sucked and call to you. My other hand grips where your sperm is concentrated and my painted nails measure your pleasure. My teeth scrape and then follows the softness of my tongue that tastes you greedily. I eagerly suck you and you are living only by the extremity of yourself which I abuse with hungry desire. I also whisper to you acidic and honeyed words that make you heady. The ecstasy lasts and you forget your self facing this world that only my feminine instinct can make you discover. This so common and so discussed gesture, I will know how to make it unique for you, and I will be dazzled by the outpouring of your intense pleasure that will find refuge in my throat, on my mouth which boasts of this extreme shininess, on the tips of my breasts and on my silky belly which will receive this heat as the most voluptuous of your presents. Everything in me will tremble because I bought you to what is the most beautiful thing in human nature — the sharing of happiness.

He had told me that he had particularly liked my phrase, "My mouth will boast of this extreme shininess." I guess that this evocative picture is already very exciting for a man, but I added to it a concept, a principle, to which he was not insensitive — I was proud to have his sperm on my lips. This is the truth, but I chose this word also because of its phonemes and poetic semantics, gracious and unexpected in the context.

As well, when I wrote to him, "I want to shine for you." I let him know that way that I wanted to be so beautiful to the point of sparkle only for him and only because of him. He confessed to me that he appreciated the expression finding it "not so bad". All of this brings me to the following observation— men sometimes need to cover a certain lack of confidence with the golden look that a woman gives to them. The terminology doesn't reflect completely my thoughts. I feel that the nuances of "confidence" are much more subtle. The couple made with love is for me a balance that balances.

In another context, I knew that he saw me correctly as an expert of what we clinically call fellatio. He confessed to me that on one hand it pissed him off, because according to him, it was clear I was trained on more than one male. But, on the other hand, he added, "I enjoy it because you excel at it." I love to practice this art as he correctly observed, but I was unable to express it fully with him. Usually I add a few personal touches which are greatly appreciated, but I didn't have any chance to make him discover this. It is all about a question of moment, of tempo, of the blue note. What is the goal in itself of an act of love? To give pleasure and to receive pleasure. I know very well how to do both for our shared delight. It took place, now being an empirical concept, having escaped again from the virtual world.

That all our shared fantasies and daydreams were able to settle so naturally and in so little time into our lived-life, seemed to me a rarity to emphasize. This must have been written someplace in our destiny.

HE SHE THEM
"We can go no further."

Apnea Pause . . .

POETRY HARMONY
EIGHTH SYMPHONY

EUCHARIST

EVERYTHING WAS ONLY SYMBIOSIS,
SYMPHONY OR SYNTAX
AND ALSO
HEAVY BREASTS FULL OF MEANING
BREASTS FOR THE SENSES
WET WITH COLOGNE
AND AESTHETIC KISSES

INTIMATE DIVING
EYES AND CARESSES
TO THE ULTIMATE CENTER
DELICACY.

MOUTH OF SUPREME WATER
LIPS APPLIED
PLEASURE DISTILLED
ALONG THE ERECTED DESIRE
EXTREME VOLUPTUOUSNESS

CHALICE-DELIGHT
UNION-COMMUNION
TUNED BODIES
ACCOMPLICE THOUGHTS.

EVERYTHING WAS ONLY SCARLET
A MUTUAL FUGUE THAT SUDDENLY BURSTS
BEYOND US, BIRTH IN THE OTHER.
ALMOST TO FAINT OR TO DIE.
LIFE TRANSFERRED.
THE FEMININE IN HIM FEELING THE MASCULINE IN HER.

COMPLETENESS INFINITUDE FULLNESS

THE RARITY OF THE MOMENT GIVES BIRTH A FEELING
OF BREATHLESSNESS AND OF WORDS BORN FREE
OF THE UNITED UNISON OF SENSUAL HARMONY
HE WAS HER SHE WAS HIM, RELIGIOUSLY UNITED
IN AN EPITOME OF THE EUCHARIST.

>WE CAN GO NO FURTHER<
WERE HIS WORDS OF THE MOMENT.
WITH A SIXTH SENSE SHE KNEW FOREVER
THAT THIS SENTENCE HAD TWO MEANINGS.

From: **FB**
To: Liz

Appeasement. Turning within. Memory of words, of the dreamed scenes, of the poems of flesh. Lightening. Suspension...

Another word that begins with an "a" and flowers in me, "amour".

From: **FB**
To: Liz

A sublime gesture that crosses my mind — your beautiful breasts heavy with desire, already stiff peaks highlight your purple underwear, laid gently on my eyelids. I experience the infinite sweetness, volume, meaning when I beat my eyelashes on the erect nipples. And when you bring them to my lips, they become so big that they fill my sucking mouth and you faint with pleasure. On my cock, oversized because of your kisses and caresses on the most sensitive spot which you've identified, you slip the heel of your extreme stilettos — pure beauty. I take it away from your foot shaded with the refined grey of your tights and bring it to my mouth to moisten. And then, with it, I gently caress your intimate lips. Bright, burning of your femininity, and you come again. Fantasies? Yes, aesthetic and sensual delight. Claimed. And soon reality, what you just described as "supreme delight, shared happiness." What do you think about that?

A novel caress that gave me intense pleasure, delight beyond expectation. Total ownership of my body only to him who could make use of it at his will.

From: FB
To: Liz

You are beautiful from everywhere. Yours, all.

With him I felt that way.

From: FB
To: Liz

How could it not be that until now our story has remained virtual? However, it has certainly been fueled with fantasy and also with a real exchange. Not to mention the sublimated images which populate our dreams and the poems that mutually inspired us. From you I do not only appreciate your magnificent cleavage, even if your naked breasts reflect in fact a way of belonging to the world. See you soon Liz.

I considered my breasts very differently since that phrase.

From: FB
To: Liz

I loved the purple, the black, and above all the poem — it is one — around a gesture of love. [. . .] Thoughts . . . chosen! Yours, all.

From: FB
To: Liz

I forgot. I adore the ointment of love that flows in abundance from the heart of your being. This is the most intoxicating of liquors. I drink the whole with sips. It will spring from your source to me, to collect in my mouth. It is a sacred gesture.

From: **FB**
To: Liz

Intimacy, secrecy, femininity: the object is so beautiful. I knew your pink color that my kisses and my cock will turn to scarlet. Your clitoris has talked to me for weeks. I kiss and kiss, and caress and erect it. I want your perfectly modeled golden brown fleece and this mole protecting the sanctuary. Your beautiful secret is sacred. I am enchanted by this voluptuous narrowness which surrounds my cock with love, sucked by your intimate lips and their fluid ointment as divinely as your mouth. How I long for this other sacred gesture, your long nails caressing and half-opening for me, my eyes, my mouth, my penis, the doors of your intimate voluptuousness. Your gestures of pleasure are the work of an artist also, refined, intense, elegant I would say, and above, all hugely exciting.

All these actions I have invented for him, just for him. Essence art which erects his senses.

From: **FB**
To: Liz

I am taking everything of you Liz. I kiss your ankles and your 6 inch heels — a minimum for you. I tremble while admiring your goddess legs. I admire your dress, too much for everything, worn with just a g-string. And then in the secret of our bedroom, you change yourself in front of me. You put on your smoked nylons and your dark blue garter belt, you chose other exciting pumps and a triumphant bra that surrounds your breasts and their erected nipples.
As if we invented, created only for us. This is called art. I've always thought that you were an artist, haven't I? I can feel it. I know it, by the words and by the love that merge in intimacy. And on top of your beauty and your figure, lies your pure soul.

Purity of the soul and rarity of a feather. Rapture of a woman and foaming of the heart.

From: FB
To: Liz

I drink your mouth.

He could. For him I was an oasis.

From: FB
To: Liz

Liz, the embodied image of desire. You are incredible, incomparable in sensuality. Your mouth opens on eternity. Your mouths. Sometimes I doubt that these wonders are promised to me, and exclusive. What a maddening wardrobe! What an art of staging love. Magnificent.

From: FB
To: Liz

What seriousness of your visage! A disturbing contrast between your sex appeal and depth of your expression. Between the provocation of your apparel — O the skirt slit up to the garter belt. And the melancholy of your eyes. I remember our meeting. You caught me right away by your mystery, not by what you offer to me now — this inexhaustible erotic imagination. I was struck that you accept the conversation, that you incite me to talk, that you seem so focused on our words. Your look was so intense and never left mine. Could I imagine the assumed wonder of femininity that you conceal under your ironic attention? I have not even glimpsed your breasts, your legs. I just took your hand for a moment, your nails being natural, and I loved the design of

your lips. I wish you wet for me much as I stand erect for you. I'm not worried. It does. Does it not?

My sex is constantly crying his absence. And again and again my love ointment is distilled in the folds of time.

Wonder of femininity, mystery, adored design of lips.

Perception of being beyond the windows.

Only to him could I appear that way.

From: **FB**
To: **Liz**

I cannot sleep, haunted by your pictures. The last one, and the most maddening of all of them, a close-up, does justice to the design of your lips, your outspread hair, the perfect painting of your nails. And, above all, the extreme tension of the garter belt on your thighs, veiled in black, and the splendor of your generous cleavage, in gentle sensual contrast which we both love. It's you, Liz, this juxtaposition of the very soft and the extremely hard. I'm missing your legs and their long perfect shape. You spoke about tears, love juice and sperm. Do not forget the juice of our mouths that will shine on your tits and my cock. It is also sacred. You are the most beautiful, the most exciting, the most sexy.

For him I was ready to be an alcove, an icon, a priestess, a peninsula, a sorceress, extreme, ardent.

From: **FB**
To: **Liz**

You are light. You are the most alive and also the most abstract. A work of art and a work of flesh. Hauntingly sublime.

I was a sacred iris and reflected light in his eye. To get lost as hauntingly sublime.

To tattoo his skin to remain hauntingly sublime.

From: **FB**
To: **Liz**

Once the blood exudes from your body it becomes nectar. But I offer you my sperm and I quaff the scented cream of your pussy.
I hunger and I thirst for you. I am fighting. I can write. I strive for fluidity. Beautiful words that you choose very well (but "to shine for me" is a well turned phrase: you are an artist). Your fluids delight. I drink all of them, even the most intimate. I'm proud to desire them.
The lost words, I will find them again. I spoke to you like never before of the poem of your soul, of our meeting comparable to the one between Apollinaire and Lou. The act of faith that I detect in the extreme tension of your nylons, and the splendor of your spring pouring out of your black lace. Liz, like 'a thing of beauty, is a joy forever' (Keats), poet of love for whom sex is a sacred altar where I regenerate myself. Softness, tenderness, passion, our words, our own words, our own actions, henceforth, won't it be? Yours, all.

Object of beauty, eternal delight" for him yes. Softness, tenderness, passion: bouquet of love vased at the altar of our unions.

These words, our words, were our only gesture. These gestures, our gestures, remain my only words.

From: **FB**
To: **Liz**

I have your last message in my heart and in my sex, I will know it by heart henceforth.

From: **FB**
To: **Liz**

I'm running. I'm running today and at every moment I want you more and more. My body surprises me. Do you see what I mean? Talk to you soon.

From: **FB**
To: **Liz**

Yes, I know that I know how to make you come like nobody has ever done, never. I will succeed tomorrow, for this too. I will fuck you with passion.

Successful substitute.
He knew how to fuck me passionately.
The tense of the past is troubling my tense of the present.

From: **FB**
To: **Liz**

O dear, thank you for your sentimental diary. I can actually feel the sweet taste of your melting mouth in mine. Sex is haunting me, sometimes hardly, sometimes tenderly. You are the aim, the focus, the furnace. I love it. Send me new photos, I miss other angles. Yours, so much.

Adored muse, temptress water nymph, furtive image.

From: **FB**
To: **Liz**

I claim my taste for talking about your supreme attraction. You provide me with visions, dreams, expectations, excitement. I'm healing you, you say? You are invading me, I feel alive and sexy.

You offer to me exceptional words. Camphorous balm. Volute of sublime voluptuousness. To invade you — softly delirious.

From: **FB**
To: **Liz**

I buy it all, your chapter one, my most! Later in the day, I will proceed to an enriched chapter two on your own selected basis. Let me confess how proud and dignified I feel to inspire such a loving sophistication. Maybe you will explain, one day, which intuition made you notice me. My staring at you seems pretty logical. Was the reverse equally expectable?

The intuition of love doesn't explain. Magical looks. Then, that it could die is despair.

From: **FB**
To: **Liz**

With you, Liz, love is but a poem of words, of gestures, of thoughts. Not only does it bring together all our senses. It also upsets our grounds, making us tumble and swoon in an unknown world of feelings, where past and present mix up with dreams. [...] appears as a beginning as well as a completion, an earthly vision of the utmost. At this moment, the hardest part of me enters the softest part of you, we think we're dying with pleasure. We are.

We did . . . Indeed that's what happened. The ornamental formulation of our two sexes envisioned made me tremble with voluptuousness.

However . . .

From: Liz
To: FB

I read all our mail today. The draft of our sublimated spiraling feelings is very perceptible. It also deciphers the friction of the characters followed by the rubbing of skins.
Also present in our mail — a fine and transparent discovering of heart and body. And an elaborate writing made of arabesque images and transcendent words.
The almost candid freshness and the strength of completely new love which wakes up the soul of the young years, are piercing there. This story, which is ours and incomparable to any other, calls and questions, but is allowed to live with pleasures and fertile frustrations.
I'm impatient to have you...

And then ...

From: Liz
To: FB

Without a blink, do you plan an autumn, a winter, depopulated of Liz?

From: FB
To: Liz

Liz's book of verse! Spirited! What about your performing art? Keep me posted, it's taking place at this very moment I guess.

With the back of his hand, dismissively, everything was declined. The unique love words are uniquely in the present declension. No future for the future. A taboo topic to avoid, he frivolously reminded me.

Triplet.
Without a hitch.
An anecdote in present tense . . .

Yesterday, on the terrace of my favorite restaurant, I was dreaming of the moon, wondering if at his place it was also this beautiful orange color, when a man approached me. From the initial moment, he complemented me. First on my hands, then my clothes, my shoes and the red polish of my toenails. His gaze wandered to my breasts. I thought he knew how to appreciate the feminine with art and detail and that he was a seasoned womanizer.

When he called Californians "superficial", I came back with, "It's superficial to say that Californians are superficial." He was surprised and amused by my reply. He is a native New Yorker — I love this city — and divides his time between Russia, New York and California. He just bought a house in California because he loved the place. Though this man has three roofs, in Chinese a man under three roofs could mean what, knowing that three women under one roof means dispute?

THE ART OF WORDS
NINTH CONVERSATION

Words have infinite powers and the one who knows how to handle them becomes similarly powerful. Of course, him, he knows. Power to persuade, to wonder, to fall in love, to excite, to educate, to share, to transcend, to create, to devote, to bring to sleep, to caress and to make dream. Him, he possesses the art of words than cannot exist without deep sensitivity and without diverse knowledge. I noticed in all his emails a vocabulary usually affiliated with theology, although, while we were hearing some singers of Christ gathered on the steps of a church, he told me that he had no faith in religion. However, I observed that one of his writings concealed more than five religious terms. I found the text very beautiful as usual and so I didn't pay much attention to this initially. It was only when I met him and we discussed religion that I understood the exact content of his lexical choice. There is nothing that fills me more with wonder than my awareness of things and through him I had several revelations.

I have absolutely no attraction to any religion. I have no education in this field and my knowledge of theology is basic. I perceive the subtlety of the word "Eucharist" now only because of him. The exceptional communion that we lived there he called "The Eucharist." Transfer of bodies. I like the sound of this word and thanks to him I have touched the definition very closely.

Recently I had a very blurry dream which actually seemed more like a vision than a dream, in which I saw us sexually united. The union of our two sexes was giving birth to a star with an intense light that sealed us to each other. I'm relating this without any comment because I was and still am overwhelmed by this image.

I think that the sexual act is inherent in what is called the quest for the divine in general. Indeed, one day while watching a film showing whirling dervishes, I found myself thinking, after the comment of the narrator, that this dance was created to be closer to God, that the action is repeated until the result is joy and well being. I thought that, in fact, it is a quest for the divine.

Whether it is about whirling dervishes, prayers, mantras, certain acts of religion repeated and redundant — like nods — the songs, the rhythm, mandalas and coitus, these are transcendental acts.

One question: have we sunk into a role play so powerful, since supported by fantasy at every moment due to the form of the communication utilized, that it brought us to the extreme ecstasy guided by the brain alone? Or, are we real halves united with mystery? Or, do we just feel a desire and a shared love? Too common a description for such a sensation. Love is a word before being a concept.

Another revelation of a different kind was coming from him and when I think about it, it moves me against my will. Very early, when I was eighteen years old, I decided not to have children. Many reasons for this — difficult childhood, no familial example, and also precise and critical observation of couples with kids. Despite my own young age, I was absolutely sure that this decision would be the best one that I could make for myself. My great paternal grandmother, whom I very much resemble, died in childbirth when she was in her thirties. I learned this when I was in my thirties. This spread like an echo into all the fibers of my body already so reluctant to the idea of maternity. Even my husbandS — and this plural is consecutive due to this irrevocable decision in me — didn't know how to convince me. Even the heavy familial and social pressure didn't convince me either. I kept my course inflexible and inexpugnable.

Despite my age I'm still fertile, yet he told me that he was touched by that. I didn't understand why, but he had this simple sentence, "It may give life."

I never thought in those terms as surprising as it may seem as it is a pure simplicity.

The word "life" in his mouth had a deep connotation for me, probably because of what he meant by it and what I could perceive. Never before had I made a link between having a child and creating life, unthinkable as it may seem. At least his art of words touched me and lighted me differently.

Lighted differently, I was on the way to look at my body and live it. He revealed the woman in me in a different light because of his spontaneous and natural remarks made when we were making love. He would have said when "we were fucking". These words no longer sound vulgar to my ears. He allowed me to discover myself as a lover in a way no other man had ever done before. This and so many other things. He knows which ones. That's why I will never forget him and he was once again right. Those three days are "unforgettable".

INTERMEZZO
FOR AN ALTER EGO

From: FB
To: Liz

I recall I actually could NOT drag my eyes away from yours, intensely wishing to catch your attention. I can swear I never experienced such an immediate attraction and tension. And no doubt, if you had remained in […] that night, we would have made love. Not only did I never stare at anyone the way I did with you, but it is the first and only circumstance when I KNEW you were expecting me.

When I read this email I received it as an electric shock. Was it his proven intelligence or his acute perception of my remarks that led him to this conclusion? Or did I route him myself on this track considering, in fact, that I was expecting a man? This hypothesis fits the mold of the rational and I think likely possible. However, a mysterious part remained. When I re-read my last emails just before this answer, I came to believe that the element of mystery would become part of the game. Too bad, but logical, although my brain is wired "anti-math" (an ugly but evocative term). I am literally a literary person who loves to dream and not to calculate and therefore find it difficult to understand logic. So I prefer to believe this element of mystery. It is too good. It is too beautiful. Note: his first emails also provided assurance regarding this inevitable attraction and belonging, without me influencing anything.

Besides, I received his confidences . . .

From: **FB**
To: Liz

I know you Liz. It is easy to be attracted by your charm and sex appeal, however discreet it may be, like when we met. But how did you read me? What made you think I was someone to listen and talk to? I would never boast about my love abilities. It does not exist per se, it is a matter of whom you care for. Then you may reveal your intimate self. You inspire me so much that I wish, I know I could please you. Give and share the most intimate and secret jubilation. In this respect indeed, you're right, nature has been extremely generous to me. I long for letting you check, what you've obviously guessed already . . .

From: **FB**
To: Liz

A stormy, rainy day. The type of weather I like most. *Raindrops Keep Falling On My Head:* you remember the song. It's all wet, declining light, wet atmosphere. Landscape blurred. Concentrated on my thoughts and dreams, the sexiest, the most dramatic visions I ever gave shelter enter and haunt my inspiration. I don't remind the way I looked at you, I just recall I could not prevent my eyes from focusing on yours. Then, it all started, unless it had begun already but we had no conscience of it yet. Beyond ourselves, beyond our will and wish. What do you think?

It had been described to me in great detail the man who is somewhere destined for me or for whom I am destined. Among other things I know that sexually he is absolutely on the same wavelength as me, and well built.

I felt it when I saw him for the first time. That's it. Nothing else to say. Just to accept it as a fact.

I actually kind of "recognized" him. Inexplicable, it was just from the feelings. That he wrote about that disconcerted me. Because this time, when he wrote me this, there was no email from me in advance that could lead him in this direction.

Today he is far away from me, physically and mentally, so what to think? Love diluted in the ocean, evaporated into the blue air, or faded in the sun? Nothing left about us . . .

He corresponds a lot to the man who was described to me. And recently he just added another correspondence although our correspondence has dried up. Desert of words and deserted feelings. I don't want to cling to the irrational. If there existed a destiny between us, it will reveal itself, as he says, "beyond ourselves, our will and our desire", and experience has shown me that he was always right. I remember as we walked, I delicately outlined our future in a rather negative way, saying that we would never see each other again. He brushed it away saying, "Don't talk about what you don't know."

So . . .

I am expecting this man, my man, the one whom I was told about long ago, described so accurately on all levels. I know already so many things about him and I'd been living in his wake for so long that I have the impression I know him perfectly. I have reached a point of wisdom and I am no longer in a hurry, letting myself float on the river. All my life I had to solicit (the term doesn't suit me but it is appropriate) to mate. Since I left my last husband, I decided not to move an eyelash. The one who wants me and who I like will come forward and come what may.

This is the case with the last three men in my life, although I think the very last that I met two weeks ago doesn't please me. "An encounter of the third kind" with the third man since I reclaimed my freedom. He approached me on his own so I gave him a chance. If I do not like him, he will know it very soon. I have no time to lose.

Regarding the two last men who probably are not my man, I knitted with them memories for my very old days and I regret absolutely nothing of those two stories. These two love affairs were both very unique, fundamentally different but related in some ways. I consider them worthy of narration because they were enchanted. They came about by a combination of the most improbable circumstances, but they really occurred. Those two last men of my life, although I met them on my territory, live in exactly the same space of geographical and professional life in another territory. They also have exactly the same place of work.

Another twist of fate — I entered in contact with one on the day of his birthday, and I went out of the life of the other . . . on the day of his birthday. Both of them the same month. There were a lot of other coincidences between those two love stories that I'm relating in another book. Contrary to what one might think, I am not one of those enlightened beings misled by a way of thinking prone to believe in mystical darkness. There is nobody more grounded than me in the basic and tangible reality of the earth. Those who know me very well can affirm this, as they rely on my clear perception and correct analysis to help them better understand their lives. I view life with an uncommon acuity. None of its details escape me. I feel coincidences, like a wink, are to be read and deciphered. The professional field common to those two men became somewhat also mine. And absolutely nothing about this was foreshadowed. Warning in the form of repetition. Maybe . . .

And the love of my life then? I thought and still think he is the one, in spite of life, in spite of everything, in spite of the evidence. It is difficult for me, even inconceivable, to dispose of such a sentiment.

And he speaks about it . . .

From: FB
To: Liz

Darling, what's happening between us carries a name. Let's not be afraid by words. Mine and yours are made of the same feeling. I am also worried of our computer disconnections. I did not get your photos. Please try again, I'm getting mad!

From: FB
To: Liz

Our love story sounds like a fairy tale. No other woman talked to me the way you do, referring so easily to more than intimate datas. It is my honor to realize you dress up just for me, make yourself even more attractive and sexy while you keep me in your thoughts.

From: FB
To: Liz

I keep your image (the last one you sent, my favorite) with me, your loving words too. Maybe I emphasized your style which corresponds with my tastes so narrowly. But we had not met yet when you purchased those stockings, those bras, those stilettos: such is your way, such is mine also.
I wish I could drench my thirst from your moistened burning lips, all of them, and nourish your desire with my most intimate liquor.

From: **FB**
To: **Liz**

You inspire me, this is probably the one reason why I want you so much. True, I love using and reading love and lust words with you. I guess you too: one always transfers one's own feeling to the other! Now you impersonate sex for me — "sex" in the English meaning, far more extensive than in French — you mention me looking at you intensely, let me reply that your reverse looking at me was not less intrusive! I did insist on your intimate self portrait: was not I right, since you eventually wrote down the most delicate and inspiring love rime I could dream of? [...] It's 10 am, I go on working and thinking of gorgeous Liz . . .

Yes. Certainly, but even if our tastes match, even if our love is like a fairy tale, it abruptly ended upon my return accompanied by my faithful and pertinent suitcase to my own land. Sudden return to the earth in the most down to earth sense. This suffering, that I decided to master, hit me right in the heart with unexpected force. A future that previously had appeared in a virtual manner, appeared in reality. No more writing, no more emotion, no hope. A great gulf which I became aware of. A big suffering despite my resolution.

Then the need to turn to other thoughts . . .

I still think that I'm overly anticipating this man of my life, but without him I feel a slow decay. He has to come soon. I live poorly without him, but I take this opportunity to polish and prepare myself only for him. However, Mr. Guitry is whispering to me, "He is late, that means he will come."

I learn. I travel. I master more and more different languages. You never know if he comes from far away. I metaphysical,

I philosopher, and I open up my mind. I listen, I read, I converse, and I reap all the knowledge and all the knowledges, all the skills, all the competencies, and also I'm learning Man — to talk Man, to understand Man, to anticipate Man, to fulfill Man — a curious language that I master better and better. After Chinese and Latin, Man is relatively simple.

As for my body and my look, I make the most of it. I use for the best what nature gave me and I work deeply on the masculine delights — the skin, the eyes, the mouth, the boobs, the butt, the hands with their long nails, the silhouette, the makeup, the attire, and the underwear, the shoes (pumps, high-heels, boots), gait, facial expression, voice, and also the enthusiasm, energy and art of love. Besides, I'm always on time, rarely do complain, do not blame but discuss. I am full of gentleness and attention. And also I love deeply.

Here is a picture of an almost geisha! Almost, as unfortunately I do not play any instrument to perfection. Regarding the rest, even though vain, everything is true. I wrote it and I repeat it — this truth is the cornerstone of this book. It is a confession that relieves. My defects, I keep them to myself and sometimes I find them funny.

So, when I compare myself to all those women around, I find myself extremely rare — a word that I want neutral, just an assessment without any judgement, either positive or negative.

I support myself, ignoring material security. I have only the money I earn. I go alone to restaurants or bars and go out alone. I drive for hours — which I adore. I work with inspiration at night and I don't really give a fig about what anyone thinks of me. I love solitude and company. Above all, I love my freedom and, then, I know how to respect that of others. There is no worse poison than intruding on the space of others and disrespecting their secret gardens.

So, I'm ornamented, prepared and repaired to embrace my destiny.

I know that our commingling will be intellectual and sexual, with sophistication and finesse. I know that a look at each other will suffice. I know that we are identical and complimentary. I know that we will draw strength and energy from each other. I know he will tame me and make me his. I know that even absent we will be present for each other and that our past will forge us strongly, to ground for our future.

For him I will be superlative and I will fulfill him and love him.

Then he wrote . . .

From: **FB**
To: **Liz**

You speak English. I answer in French. Do I deserve the type of love you think for me? . . . Not in French — unconsciously. Now I really answer in French. De quelle manière mériterais-je d'être aimé?

As I was suggesting — writing in English instead of French to mask the emotion — that maybe nobody knew how to love him at his fair value.

He answered with this unexpected almost monosyllabic phrase that filled my heart with deep emotion:

From: **FB**
To: **Liz**

But you, indeed you know, I know it already.

Why in the world did he tell me that? Probably always playing the same game previously referenced — but to play like that is not to play.

What else? Only he has the answer. I gave up any theories,

shunted on the road to the truth by my deep desire. Too much heartache.

Yes I do know that I know how to love him, as this is very natural for me. I do not expend any effort. This sentence of his, the simplest, the shortest, is engraved in my soul, and chanted in my mind as it speaks to me.

The reality still shades its truth without qualms. And does not stop me from thinking that he played (movie, play, novel) a role. A role that involves no consequences in real life, such as a Greek theater mask that will be removed to sleep. Yet! Why did he enunciate this idea that I knew how to love him if this had no meaning for the future?

The rational . . .

He just needed to escape, to know he could seduce a woman he found attractive and desirable and to possess her.

"And if she hangs on?" A line from the movie *And God Created Woman.* He was intelligent enough to know how to end the relationship with honor and elegance. This is what he did.

The irrational . . .

What I fundamentally liked in him: his authenticity, his underlying simplicity, his naturalness, and . . . his weaknesses. What we shared made us complicit with each other, incomparable to others, as if we had known each other for a long time. With him I felt myself, totally comfortable, and it has been like that since the first second I met him. I think he shared this feeling. He shared with me the intimacies of his life, details like the soles of his shoes being too slippery in the rain. He shared with me the contents of his professional interviews. We discussed the way he dressed and he showed me his new clothes. He commented how valuable a tie could be when it was full of memories. He was looking for a new watch, gluing our four eyes to the display window of the jewelry store. All of this with a great confidence in me, like a couple of friend-lovers.

What prevailed then? . . .

An innate connivance or a complicity born after four months of intense and deep exchanges?

He confessed to me also, "Nobody ever took care of me like you did."

I became aware of this in a number of little details. He appeared to me to be in a solitude that left him completely alone in dealing with everything that makes the everyday life. In another way I think that a man of his standing, having a role to play in front of the audience which required a mastery of every second, needed a break from time to time, needed to be finally himself without pretending, without giving special attention to everything he does or says. I offered him this interlude. One image illustrated completely my claim. Wearing only white underwear, on all fours, he pushed out of the bedroom the tray with the leftovers of our recent dinner. This image is still a continuing memory and brings a tender smile to my lips. Once again he touched me, probably despite himself.

One evening, in a bathrobe sitting casually on the leather chair facing me, his posture suggesting he was perfectly at ease, with his cell phone he called one of his probably very close friends. The conversation he had with him then, and obviously he didn't want to hide anything from me, held my attention. Indeed, he was evoking . . . love and he asked about the path of that feeling in the life of his friend. "And how goes your love life?" I received those words as a breath of fresh air! So throughout life, in any context, love remained a major concern. My lovers in general, usually being twenty years younger than him, did not have that spontaneity, that candor and enthusiasm about love. He caressed my heart. Once again, he made me aware of a fact that I was pleased to discover. Love is beyond everything and imperishable, ignoring all contingencies.

Then the conversation turned to the "object" of that love. "It's a pity because she has it all and I thought it would work. She is beautiful, intelligent, elegant and she is brilliant in her work. Etc. etc. etc." He was full of praise. I wish he could consider me in that way. But the facts that he lays in front of me without modesty, made me think that he was quite likely to notice all of this in a woman.

I discovered also that we shared certain core values of life. I love being at once the lover, the friend, the confidante, the muse, providing a little maternal support, devotion and dedication, and I could feel that he had a great need for this woman of many faces to whom he could give expression to every facet of his profound self. I admired him, and this opened for him all the powers, and all I discovered in him delighted me and made me full of love with tenderness. I was very sensitive to his remark when, preparing my suitcase for my coming departure and my dresses no longer merged with his clothes in the closet, he said that he found his closet sad and not so pretty as when my sexy dresses and "frilly" underthings kept company to his suits.

Our encounter had a meaning, but perhaps only for me.

However, I want to make a presumption and allow myself to describe the encounter from his point of view. I'd softened his torment with dreams and helped divert him from reality when a tragedy occurred in his life exactly two months after our first exchange of emails.

Regarding my interpretation of our encounter, I thought I recognized him. It is true I was waiting for him. Inexplicable attraction above all, uncontrolled and above all uncontrollable.

What makes me sad is that our subtle perception of each other became tangible, equaling everything that we conceptually imagined in all its extremeness. *But he said it himself . . .*

From: **FB**
To: **Liz**
You fit my dreams, and I'm a dreamer. I want you.

And yet, what is the principle of a dreamer?
Only to dream.
Prove me the contrary my love . . .

CHAPTER PRETEXT
STUDY OF THE TEXT

From: FB
To: Liz

My lovable love-loving love, I also went powerless in the last 24 hours, hence my non replying to your two last love filled messages. I can hardly breathe, so deadly is the core of those scenes you offer me. Never in my life, in my past, in my readings could I imagine that a woman of your charm and femininity might think and describe so explicit love scenes just for me. Of course, I buy them all, at your pace, at your convenience, I let myself be guided by your adorable intuition. Let me ask you one question: did another man inspire you the way I do? Of course, I hope you deny, since I would feel outrageously jealous of whomever else. I told you about my own doubts, you appeased them partly. I am definitely upset by this love celebration you conceive for me, this attention to intimate details, the length of your high heels (6 inches), that of your stockings: how I crave for your ever so long legs no ordinary nylon can actually fit! Do you realize how sexy are your words and thoughts and attentions? You make me feel even more sensual and charm filled. To be honest, I know I can please, my mind is a strong asset. You see me as your lover, I approve, I swear, I pledge I am. I can't be more yours than I am now. Until we meet again, of course.

This writing from him went directly to my heart because it summed up everything that made our story. I also admit that I felt in it sincerity that touched me. This writing follows an evocation of how I will dress for him, to be sexy and desirable just for him. I was in front of my mirror trying on all these different erotic outfits that I bought recently, just for him again, to see if I liked them enough, when it occurred to me to share these moments with him. I'm dreaming of a man who can be interested by all those details and concerns that make up the daily life of a woman. A man who can give his opinion and discuss all these sensitive issues. Sharing in each occasion is sublimation for me. Innocently, I really wanted him to approve my choices and to direct me and to express to me what he would have liked or what was not tasteful to him. I knew he had a keen sense of aesthetics. I deliberately use the term innocent to answer his question:

From: **FB**
To: **Liz**

Do you realize how sexy are your words and thoughts and attentions?

Very sincerely the answer is no . . .

It is normal — still the term normal doesn't suit me, because normal features different standards — to be attractive and seductive for a man that counts. I am made for that and there are no limits. And he counted and still counts. I was obeying this pure desire to please him with the underlying notion to give him as much pleasure as possible by offering him what seems important in a man's eyes: a woman's body dressed for love and exciting desire. And I wanted it only because I thought that was what he expected of me and that suited me perfectly. Here is the innocence — according to me a woman must work to fulfill the taste of her partner, of the man she prefers among others, otherwise where would be the special consideration of this man relative to others?

Without any sexy attention it would have been like offering a present that had not been properly giftwrapped and without a bow.

No one else but him saw me in the attire that I invented and created for him. It is the same for the words and the thoughts, arranged carefully just for him. Does he realize that? Apparently not, because he stated that he couldn't imagine that and had never lived it, hence my boomerang question: "Had any one every been able to love him for his true value?" Me, I know how to read him and I know his true value, consequently I know how to love him and I know intrinsically that he needs me. His writings are shouting it.

The expression "breathtaking" became clear to me when I had the opportunity to experience it in my discovery of the Grand Canyon. That's exactly what I felt in front of such immensity, liberty and beauty. I find it flattering that he made this mention about me. Because of blatant lack of love and compliments, I took and I take all his incantations. **"My love, lovable loving love"** — four loving words at once. Unexpected!

I take also the description, **"I can hardly breathe."** He was offering me minty balm for my wounds which do not heal.

Again, jealousy scratched — **"I would feel outrageously jealous of whomever else."** — has no reason to be. The past is ashes and embers, the fire does not heat anymore. My men have inspired my attitudes towards love. This I do not deny, but he put his finger on a crucial point — never ever like him, never ever like with him.

To summarize, maturity, lack of love, a profound sensitivity, and the uniqueness of our relationship, led me to this depth of feeling, and these are important factors, but his essence was to be unique. Although he doubted himself greatly, this was very difficult for me to understand because in my case, for survival reasons, I cannot afford self doubt. This strength can be learned and can be mastered when understood. The appearance, I leave it to the "superficials" and to the "narrows". Mine, although enviable, is often difficult to live with and doesn't always bring me the best. So, it is a tie.

From: **FB**
To: **Liz**

I told you about my own doubts, you appeased them partly.

Very happy that I knew how to erase his doubts about his appearance. I would have known how to erase them completely if given time. The proof, **"You make me feel even more sensual and charm filled."** He wrote this sentence after only a few weeks of correspondence.

From: **FB**
To: **Liz**

To be honest, I know I can please, my mind is a strong asset.

To please with the intellect is necessary but insufficient. I write this directly, like a sneeze. The charm lies elsewhere. The intellect, coupled with a sensitivity, gives rise to humor, a sense of irony and self-mockery. The intellect coupled with an aesthetic eye, gives way to pleasure and good taste. The intellect, coupled with imagination, melts into the artistic. The intellect, coupled with sensuality, links to a sophisticated erotic vocation. The intellect, coupled with chosen and lived experiences, leads to tolerance and altruism. Because the intellect by itself can sometimes be boring, it is not appropriate to set it on an equal level to appearance. Appearance, which is cultivated only in order to seduce, is coupled to very little. I truly believe that he had all these "liners" that I just mentioned that flesh out the mantle of his ego, making it cozy and comfortable to wear.

From: **FB**
To: **Liz**
You see me as your lover, I approve, I swear, I pledge I am.

Once again, I only told him that I saw him as my lover because that was what he was expecting from me and what I wanted to offer to him. He pleased me, he attracted me from the first moment. I love my impulses and my initial impressions when I see a man for the first time. Generally, I'm not wrong. I don't make mistakes. I know what will happen, even if I don't control anything. I could have never contacted him.

From: **FB**
To: **Liz**
I can't be more yours than I am now. Until we meet again, of course.

At the time he wrote this email, I wanted to feel this sense of **"I cannot be more yours."** "Yours" is a possessive pronoun that echoes the possessive adjective "mine" at the beginning of the text and I truly believe that in fact he was, at that precise moment, at the peak of giving himself to me — gift of love.

From: **Liz**
To: **FB**
You, I live you subliminally. It is the first word that comes to me. No other man matters. There is only you. For me it is clear and

simple. I told you already, I have a lot to offer and be sure that everything is for you. And I tell you that, once again, I am very, very different. You will learn me. If you don't mind, answer me just three words before I fall asleep. You please me and not only for your intellect.

Rereading my text I realized shortly what I had actually written. I'm very altruistic and I'm always careful not to overwhelm others by my demands, that I minimize here by saying, "Answer me only three little words." I realize long after what those three words were . . .

ABOUT FEELING
LOVING-MAGNET
CHAPTER

His words, my slaves, built two fortresses — a protective enclosure and a second Taj Mahal. His words, my pigeons, have been transformed into symbolic doves. His words gave me coffers of secret jewels to adorn my moments of solitude, my woman's nudity.

This is to fill the tender poetess who sleeps in my heart. More prosaically, I was receiving his messages with jubilation and heart shaped iris.

I had a sinking heart at the hotel there with him. At home, I had boundless energy. I rushed to my computer as soon as I crossed the threshold of my house. I was breathing with lungs fully opened and without thinking. The sun blazed stronger than before. This love story could not flourish, even if given the full force of subtle control. But I wanted to believe in it, although the faux Braque imitation background canvas stretched out at the hotel.

I was laughing about nothing, about everything. I had a childish look and a light-hearted humor. I regarded life with wrinkled eyes . . . only because of the smile. I knew the day would come when I would be living what I'm living today — words, images, moments, scenes, atmospheres, streets and the hotel, under a form of remembrance that my faithful memory would distill in my head and in my heart. Awareness quickly changed after the plane ride. Of course we will see each other again. I think of him constantly. He became my constant companion — of my head and of my life. Oh well, five minutes during which I didn't think about him . . . and all these other men, they annoy me so much. They cannot even see that the horizon is blocked. Damn! I just broke a nail. It will be too short. It's not possible! I have not spent a day since my return that I do no look back on this adventure in each of the forms that I mentioned before. The nights are beautiful with him. I feel alive and sated. But is he still here? I feel he is not, as he was tortured inside. I just call his name to be sure, and then I do not know what to say. "I love you" is shouting in my throat. But the evidence stuck obviously — only two days left and I'll miss you — and after what? I dare to ask him because I know . . . Oh! What despair that hair. He is really not going to like it. Too dry for sure. So oil bath and hair dresser. Let's buy another dress. Just one, and after it is over, I promise. But men don't stop looking at me! Normal. I feel beautiful and desirable. Somebody is influencing me somewhere. Only one day left. Enjoy every second of your favorite mint chocolate ice cream. It is melting so evidently. He will be in touch with you. Don't worry! Cool! I love when he speaks to me, when we speak together. After . . . we could not do it anymore. I'm leaving in two weeks. Time is going slow, slower than usual. Let's see my list. What am I missing now? Oh, those shoes. The heels take an incredible amount of room in my suitcase. Fortunately, I have a huge suitcase . . . On the plane I speak and write in Chinese. So unexpected. In the taxi I speak in Spanish to the driver. He is adorable and kind. He tells me that I'm pretty and he comments on the city, his city, in his language. I love it. I borrow his cell phone to call my waiting future lover and tell him I'm coming.

All bodes well, and his voice rings deep in my heart. I was expecting so much at this moment. Soon I will be . . . in his arms, he will be in my body. I love it!

Only two hours left. Watch him carefully. You will never live again moments like this. Today I'm joining him. I hope I don't miss the plane . . . At five o'clock in the morning there is no crowd on the freeway . . . Bye bye. What is the cleaning lady doing here? He opened the door for her, closing the door of our farewell. You know it's better that way . . .

My last touching vision of him, his manhood protruding from his underwear, darting one last time for me in front of my eyes. And his remark, "You see what I have said and written to you could not be more true. You have here the tangible evidence. Whatever, erecting for you is endemic."

Just to let you know, I have an exceptional and precise memory so every one of his words is carved in me and all his words are reconstructed here in this book with the exactitude of a Swiss watch.

If he didn't realize it then, I want him to know now how much he touched me. It was the last, most moving connivance we had, possessing a touch of the adolescence freshness of his own being in the guise of seriousness. This is the way I am too. I know him by heart. I would have loved so much to lavish him with my caresses which he liked so much. This would have provided good memories for the end point of our story. But then, I still had hope I would see him again soon.

I would have liked to share these last moments one on one with him, sex to sex with him. Two looks populate my memories — his look, somewhat embarrassed, sad, and long, as if to set a final image. So — crumpled sheet for the wastebasket my hope to see him again. And the second look was the look of the maid for whom he had opened the door of "our" bedroom. Young, pretty, of foreign origin like me. I could read in her eyes what she thought of me — a pinch of contempt with an ounce of morality. "How can you do that?" Had she taken me for a call girl or something like that. Likely. Once again the kneading of our moral education splashed me. Certainly, I had had sex for three days in a row and although he would have used "fucking", I claim to have "made love" — explaining that way to the maid the dose of sincerity she had omitted from her too quick and so stereotyped judgement.

Black eyes, cherry mouth, fishnet stockings and a miniskirt do not determine a woman. I love to play with this appearance. A primitive impression with tons of quantifiers. I use this appearance in order to discover the man who will take the time and the effort to discover my "pot of pink". In French, "pot au rose" — no "x" to "au" and no "s" to "rose" due to the etymology — we don't talk about roses in a vase, but about make-up — lipstick and pink blush erecting a bridge towards sexuality. The woman who wears them will be showing her availability. How simple.

Not for him. He knew how to see my essence, the pink of my soul. At least I believe so . . .

I fully understood that he wanted to live this story for himself, for his pleasure of course, to possess the woman he had conquered with his polished and prolific prose. So much time devoted to writing. But perhaps also a little bit for me, with the implicit sense that this story would take place only to honor a particular, parenthetical correspondence and to honor my sincerity. A whirlwind in which he was swept up and everything would have to be forgotten because it cannot be another way, due to the conjuncture.

But, strangely, most of the time after the conquest is seduced and possessed, she falls into oblivion. In this regard,

I wish to add my woman's point of view, often ignored in such situations. The man who has once been tasted, doesn't have the same appeal anymore. There exist those who make you as impatient as the enjoyment was delectable, and those who create no further urge.

Once tasted, forgotten. I expected it — just three brief days, three little turns. But the break occurred three weeks before the encounter. This is the strange fact. What I mean by breaking is the break of this golden thread that connected us strongly. Thread made with connivance of head and action, like emails exchanged in the same second, synchronized thoughts. And particularly these intimate feelings, the deep and enthusiastic presence of the other despite the physical distance. For sure, he was torn, very torn, to the point of actually not wanting to live the encounter. An awareness that the dream of our story should stay in its original condition. And, above all, an extremely strong manipulation by the counterbalance.

My hypothesis regarding the sudden drying up of this voluble love which was abruptly smothered was that he had too strong an interest in his computer, an inseparable companion even during a dinner. A tipsy look, a too loud laugh, an unusual behavior. What a pity. There is love and there is life, its enemy. Life was the winner. No feminine to that word. O.K. The life, the real one, triumphed. The life, the virtual one, remained without any voice. What a pity again, because as usual he is still right. I am the only one who knows how to love him in order to make him happy and serene.

Fortunately, he left me his magnificent writings full of sugary love. Oh good!
It was not a dream then . . .

From: FB
To: Liz

Yes, I missed you ever so much, even if you had let me expect one full day of silence. I could not make a choice between your dress codes: to be honest, I positively adore all you think of, would it be in terms of garments, of perfume, of feelings, of gestures. Everything that incomes from you fulfills a secret desire, and I have known for long that whichever word you whisper to me will sound like a love confession. I am crazy thinking both of your leather made black mini skirt and your spike heeled boots. Not a piece of your wardrobe which does not lead to fainting with passion. Of course I will join you soon, I'll tell you when. Of course I dream of you. Of course I'm actually burning with an exhausting lack of you. I do my best to proceed in my work, but the only sentences I am able to write down are Liz filled, Liz full, Liz, Liz, Liz . . .

From: FB
To: Liz

Carried along by the substantial task I assigned to myself. A very mind absorbing activity, implying concentration, silence, time elapsing. Then enters Liz, in my mind, in my heart, in my body. My sex escapes from my control and conscience, grows so big and hard, mad with desire and passion, devastating and aching. I feel I would almost cry. Rescued by literature, and expectation: your next sexy message, our next wild reunion.

From: FB
To: Liz

Do not change in any respect, please! I love you the way you are, in every aspect. I hold your breasts to my lips, kiss and bite the nipples, cover them with shining fluid, stroke them with the rim of my demanding cock. Your long red painted nailed hand holds it, presses it between your breasts, take it to your lips and tongue . . . I almost faint with delight. Would you?

I kiss your sweet lips, mingle our tongues, one of the most intimate love gestures, don't you think? (With many others I let you describe, unless we share this delightful task). The best, the sweetest, the hottest for you.

"Did you notice it?"
"What?"
"Here are your 'three little words.' There. Just after 'please.'" . . .

ALWAYS FOREVER

I n French and English he wrote me passionate texts. I really miss them now. Each of his words was a pure source of refreshment when intensely thirsty. I knew it could happen, but I didn't want to believe that the river could ever dry up. No not him! Not like all the others who disappeared from my life and left me only memories. Memories, I consider them the cemetery of the soul, and I deposit roses there that always droop. I want to live for real and with him I'm alive, so alive. All these unique and magnificent exchanges, like a mandala, a sand castle or a house of cards . . . unimaginable.

Without interposed computer, out of virtuality, to make love, to walk, to talk, to have breakfast, lunch or dinner, to laugh, even if not every day, even if it is with time limits. Even once a month like a period. I accept everything and don't want to consider the confusion dictated by the return to the other life. Why not become a call girl for him? He will call me just for his pleasure, providing mine. To take the role to its extreme, I will fulfill his every whim and desire. I would take that rather than the absolute nothing, the absolute vacuum, with reminiscences. To abstract himself — precarious words. He cannot do it. Material contingencies and resurgence of conflicts.

But still . . .

From: FB
To: Liz

I receive the strength of your tenderness. Your extreme photos tempt me madly. I am ready to receive them, to devour them, to worship them. I kiss you. And this is not the word, etymologically — I drink from your mouth the water of life.

From: FB
To: Liz

Visit to the computer, discovery of your picture: another shock. My favorite one, the little one where you're wearing a black veil concealing your underwear, also black. What a beauty! I can hardly breathe. My body writhes. The emotion grips me. I do not see enough of your face, your lips, your eyes. I have in my head two of your magnificent confessions, beginning with my first name: "F. If only you could see my breasts." And, "F. I desire you." You embellish my life and I need it.

From: FB
To: Liz

A wonderful Liz filled day: reading, starting to write, getting closer and closer to my topic. Stay close, always.

A resentment towards him developed as he wrote "Stay close always" because I'm not quite sure that he could or would meet this assertion . . .

THE VOLUPTUOUS CHAPTER
ALL HIS DESIRES
FULFILLED

24th floor / Room 2412
2nd stay of three days

DAY ONE . . .

My love program was concocted by reading and rereading his emails in order to identify all his impulses, the least of his fancies, the least of his desires for a Woman. Yes. Why capital, because there is one thing that he doesn't suspect. By a curious fact of nature, I have three times the normal amount of female hormones, which makes me very special. I explain sometimes the male attractions that I provoke by the fact that some men subtly perceive this. My ultra femininity is almost palpable.

From: **FB**
To: **Liz**

I sort of feel the incredible softness of your skin. And your secret is burning. Never did I inspire and receive such a poetic and accurate account of someone's intimacy. My feeling is that your pussy is the most accomplished and splendid part of yourself. It is a compendium of Liz's achievements, both

utterly natural and untrimmed, as well as sophisticated and so sensual. It provides visual and sexual delight to the fortunate one you agree to as your lover, not many indeed compared to the number of applicants. I dare figuring myself as the one to come. The one to whom you will allow and expect he will lift your dress, kiss your skin with passion, stare at your eyes, place his hand on your sacred bush, his lips on your inner lips, his tongue around your erected peak and swallow your spirited liquor. You make someone else of me, Liz. I take you with me deep in my heart and cock. Yours, wholly.

From: FB
To: Liz

I want you in black. Very simple pumps with crazy stiletto heels, black lingerie and black mascara, scarlet mouth and really long scarlet nails.

My nails are now long and adorned with bright red, giving to my hands a sophisticated touch, making them beautiful, long, thin and elegant. Red and black are my colors as he rightly observed. My lingerie and my simple shoes with long stiletto heels match my eyes. My scarlet mouth and scarlet nails match my sex in the grip of the oasis of desire. My skin has an irresistible softness. Compared to it, silk is like sisal and confesses to being surpassed. So many scented showers and attentive cares while thinking only of him. My fleece, as he liked to call it, is now a natural triangle and not disciplined, made of soft black curls, free and foamy, that seem to me very exciting and exults my womanhood. Sophisticated and sensual for his pleasure. To respect his descriptions I stopped visiting the beautician whose cultural background — and probably to grow her business — persuaded me to tame this part of my self, my flamboyant foliage, cutting it like a little bush from a French garden — didn't he write bush to qualify this part of me.

I feel pretty and desirable and the look of men confirms this for me. Their courting is more diligent than ever. But, he is right like always. Very few of them tasted me. I'm very picky and I need a lot of criterion to be fulfilled before lying down near or, rather, under or on top of, a masculine body. He knows for sure he is my next lover. His enunciated doubt about it is only hypocrisy wrapped in modesty.

I'm wearing a dress made with a curious mix, silk and spandex, in the shade of grey and black, fitted in the middle with a zipper, full of ulterior motives. The one who I allow to do what he wants to do was non other than him. He lifts my dress, kisses passionately the uncovered flesh above the stockings, looks at me very deeply, like a brash intruder, places his hand on the silky smooth shade of my belly, puts his lips on the most erogenous part of my privacy, rolls his tongue around my darting clit, and tastes my intimate liquor.

That he could take so much pleasure from my offering womanhood, made him, to my eyes, a wonderment. Being with him always transported me, being completely his delighted me.

From: **FB**
To: **Liz**

I thought of your breasts. Of your red kissing expert lips. Of your fascinating charcoal made up eye lashes. Above all, of your purple and dark secret. Secrets, should I write, because I dare confess I dream of your buttocks, hardly veiled in a daring black something. You love it as much as I, don't you, Liz darling? Your ass is a splendor. I'm dreaming greedily of it. I confess it without blushing.

My curves are Sahara Dunes and my sex is the Empire of the Middle ready for all the assaults, all the adoration. My perfectly poppy red lips, half opened, greedy and lusciously glistening with desire. My hair, a golden blond with a few darker strands to keep it silky, is carefully styled for him.

My lashes are long and lush, curved deep with black mascara to amplify their caresses, my eyes are Arabized with kohl, producing a rare and sensual languor. My breasts and my buttocks are contoured with unavoidable temptations.

From: **FB**
To: **Liz**

In my dreams you almost always wear black undies and stockings.
I long for your five course feast. I'd like you to concentrate on each of them. Your mascara painted eyes, and what you would do with them. Your red wet glossy mouth, your expert tongue and teeth. Your triumphant boobs, their nipples oversized with lust. Your slim waist, circled with an outrageous garter belt and black lace panty. Your divinely long shaped legs, with their stretched brown black stockings. Your round, firm, soft ass, just made for my hand and mouth. Your most attractive self, your cream filled love pussy, hardly covered or discovered by your dark string, showing your shining fur and opened purple lips. A full description of each of those love tools, and how you would play with them and me.

I wear my proven love attire, its effectiveness previously measured, and permit it to fulfill his most extreme expectations. My thong, my stockings and my shoes with stiletto heels, all in black, are impatient. My black lace shirt that elegantly surrounds and reveals, languishes on my skin. The matte black garter belt enhances the roundness of my ass.

From: FB
To: Liz

How soft your mouth is. I would have liked a close-up picture of it as well as of your eyes, your hands, your breasts. 38D now. Of your ankles, of your fleece, of your slit.

From: FB
To: Liz

Because your love making is pure, I'm sure we'd make photos of it, so as to get even more crazy for one another. I realized I had never used my imagination, fantasy, day dreams to such an extent.

When he left me by myself for a moment so that I could adorn and prepare myself for him, I presented the first act of my play. From the entrance door to the bed I spread out my black suede boots, my grey jacket and my grey and blue scarf. Also my black suede mini skirt, my cashmere sweater with a Vneck, my gloves, and . . . my camera. He made great pictures of my red and shiny wish-fulfilling lips. I opened slightly my lips and caressed them with my tongue, and I sent a kiss of breath. My fingers with their long red nails were inquisitive. He was my artistic director and looked at me with duplicate eyes: lustful and photographic eyes. Then he asked me to take his penis in my mouth and watch at the same time that he took a photo, a look at once mischievous and naughty. He wanted to save the image. Then his sperm was proud upon my lips, also immortalized by the click of the camera.

The next picture was of my hands on my breasts. He wanted the tips of my excited breasts darting between my fingers. So I caressed my breasts for him so as to offer to him a troubling show. My hands were like caressing feathers and my nipples erect like never before. Just for him.

He wanted also to seize my fine and delicate ankles —
this description is not mine, but are the words of a professional
Parisian photographer — a desire which pleased me as I
felt it reflected his artistic insight. In fact, when the Parisian
photographer asked me the favor of such a picture when I was
around twenty, he told me about the beauty and the sensuality of
my ankles. I even remember the shoes I was wearing at the time.
Dark blue pumps with stiletto heels and a little strap around
my ankles. And I remember also my gesture — I had arched
my foot in order to pick up something on the ground. He took
some pictures which I've never seen. I was not surprised by the
fact that he, so artistic and so sensitive, thought exactly the same
as this photographer. So he wanted my pumps with stiletto
heels, he wanted my ankles in the view finder, then he wanted
my entire leg covered with very thin nylons. When he arrived
at the top of my thighs, he looked at me intensively and asked
me to slowly pull down my thong so he could glimpse, and then
see, my fleece. I did exactly as he asked, sliding my long fingers
between my skin and the fabric to reveal the contrast between
the white of my skin and the black of my triangle. The faint, but
now familiar click of the camera took place and then . . . silence.

Suddenly he kissed my mouth voluptuously with his eyes
open to see mine closing and whispered in my ear the coarse
words promised in so many emails asking me to do something I
had never done before.

From: **FB**
To: **Liz**

**How I long for this other sacred gesture of yours. Your long
nails caressing and half opening for me, for my sight, for my
mouth, for my penis, the intimate door of your voluptuousness.
Your gestures are artistic also, refined, elegant, and I would
say above all, hugely exciting.**

Then I did it for him again. I readjusted my thong, opening my legs as much as possible by crunching the sheet with my heels and, with my left hand, dismissing the tiny piece of cloth that barely covered my slit. Respecting his words, I offered to two looks, his own and that of mechanics, my index finger with its long nail opening the entrance to my pussy. I lavished him with my caresses and my warmth. He did not take pictures right away this time, probably too excited by what that vision triggered in him. In fact, he put out his tongue and stroked my clit (always his own words) while his fingers dug into my hot cunt. I was melting with pleasure and I felt a river flowing into my privacy. I then understood his goal, a realistic photo showing the excitement of my sex. It would change its color from red to scarlet, and its increase in size was also quite apparent. As to the cream of my pussy, still his words, it dripped with softness around my sex, which he found beautiful, so he told me.

Its only then that he triggered the device.

Many more pictures this time.

And then other photographs and other desires . . .

From: **FB**
To: **Liz**

My vision just at this moment: your long nailed painted fingers pulling aside your drenched string, gently stroking your burning pussy.

The small little piece of black fabric that was barely covering the most secret part of me is drenched with my love water. I took this delicate piece of cloth and pulled it aside to reveal myself to his aphrodisiac look. Then I started to stroke my pussy, first for his pleasure, then for mine. My fingers move back and forth exciting the flesh already exhilarated by his kisses and his electrifying eyes. I slipped into me, and I felt both like a penis and a vagina. I licked my fingers staring into the depths of his jade iris (one of his requests by phone in a night of big excitement). Then he chose to immortalize the wave of my orgasmic spasm in the box that steals images ever faithful to the eye of reality.

From: **FB**
To: **Liz**

Yes, darlingest, please kiss me like no one ever did. I can feel your tongue snaking into my mouth, making me pant with desire. I love your wonderful tits, so round and soft, so tempting, so heavy in your mind-blowing lingerie. Yes Liz, I want to talk to you crudely, but only if you come when you read me, only if you reply in the same way, only if you fall in love with me and my cock, just like I fell in love with your lips, your lashes, your nipples, your clit.

We kissed like no one ever kissed before. Fusion of mouths, an intimated and intimate exchange, a sexual act leaving us drunk with pleasure and desire. He freed my breasts from their black lace, which gratefully acknowledged this newfound freedom by offering him the hardness of their nipples, perfectly designed for his greedy mouth. I loved the feeling of the pressure of his mouth and the fleeting bite of his teeth.

My desire became intolerable and diffused with an intense burning on my skin and on my soul. His spicy and unheard of words were not innocent to my excitation. The caresses of my eyelashes were sublime to the hypersensitive points of his anatomy. He literally possessed me, taking everything of me, and came in me. Yes I was overwhelmed and in love with him and his cock. I could feel his cum hitting deep inside me giving me a nameless pleasure. We were eager to have each other and the contact of our skin capsized us. He said, "Come my love", with an intensity in his voice. He was a theatrical lover in love with my lips, my lashes, with my breasts, with my clit. When I pointed out his loving words his swashbuckling comment was, "It came to me like that." Then he added, "I like you, you know." I thought, as an expert in love for sure. And what about the rest, my love?

From: **FB**
To: Liz

A love scene, magnificent and painful because of the absence. When we meet next, you open your door smiling. We have awaited this moment for so long. The air is filled with your perfumes. At first, you suggest a show. You would rub your lips with this cherry lipstick of yours, and make up your eyes with the dark mascara, looking both at your mirror and at me by reflection. You would take my hand in your long nailed and red lacquered hand, open your drawers and let me make a choice. I will pick up a pair of black stockings and belt, you will roll them along your sculpted legs and fix them tight, so tight to the garter. Still plunging into my eyes. Then your fingers will unveil your pussy, hardly concealed by a silk and lace undie. A black and white marvel you will slightly open. Then you'll stand, letting me hear the sensual sound of your ever so high heels on the floor. I will smile at you.

From: **FB**
To: Liz

You make up your beautiful visage (better than "face") just for me. Watching both the mirror and me in reflection. Painting your lips red, brushing your eye lashes black. Your long red lacquered nails open a drawer: which stilettos will you pick up for me? The highest heeled black ones. You slide them on,

walk a few steps: a sort of a show, letting me savor their sweet sound on the floor. Your impeccable hands slightly lift your dress, letting me see the light lace and silk undie that hardly conceals your intimacy. Your dark bush, shining. Our mouths in one another's, our love liquids melting and mingling, our tongues mixing in the most passionate kiss we ever dreamed of. My hands groping at your bra, revealing your gorgeous and hardened tits, my lips kissing, licking, biting them. So much desire it feels like a deadly pain (just like now while I'm writing to you). Then we become wild, rushing to each other's sex. I engulf the burning mount, delighting myself with your taste and fragrance, with your rushing pleasure down my throat. You capture my oversized cock, stroking the sensitive spots, sucking as much of it as you can, our private parts glow with lust and coming. What we're experiencing, we've never gone through so far. I wish you proceed, letting me know about your feelings. I have to pause for a while, my body is so aching, especially my prick devastatingly aimed at you, Liz.

After having opened the door for him, I welcome him with my best smile, telling him my joy at seeing him again after having waited so long for this meeting.

The air is slightly tinged with my perfume. I know that he is very sensitive to heavy scent. I make up for him in front of him. First my lipstick, number 18 by Yves Saint-Laurent *Rouge Volupté* that I apply sensually to my lips. I slide my lips on each other, one of the most feminine gestures, and I look at him by reflection in the mirror of the bathroom where I invited him to follow me. Perhaps it is sometimes pleasant for men to observe these intimate gestures reserved for the woman. The mascara licks my eyelashes, depositing a welcomed coat, giving character and depth to my eyes. He put on the beige marble counter one of my black stockings with my matching garter belt attached.

As I pass in front of him, my actions are fluid and sophisticated. The stockings are tight to the extreme, the way he likes, the tenseness expressing a possible break, an unexpected revelation.

I put on a beautiful pair of shoes with incredible heels whose red soles match my lipstick. He had told me that nothing would be too high and so, in fact, my heels are New York skyscrapers. His smile tells me of his appreciation.

I take a few echoing steps on the marble floor of the bathroom for his pleasure. Hearing is, I think, a sense a little behind compared to the others in exacerbating the senses for and by love. His very masculine sensibility to the sound of my heels hitting the ground intrigues and excites me in a way I never thought of before. My Eiffel Tower heels are suggesting to my hips to move with a torrid sensuality, my back arching like a feline. The dizzying heels are a miracle of eroticism.

Then I raise my dress with slow and graceful movements to offer the spectacle of silk lace barely covering my shimmering black triangle.

He kisses me with dizzying craziness. I only feel softness — the softness of his tongue, the softness of all that he wants to make me feel. This act of fusion, combining our fluids and our essences, spreads to my heart and radiates as a hot and caressing wave in the pit of my belly.

From: **FB**
To: **Liz**

I wrote to you the hottest lovingest ravagingest letter I ever thought of, so daring I was not certain not to shock you. Wrong feeling, nothing regarding passion could hurt you, is it not? I described the perceived splendor and proudness of your tits, I could but just imagine under your garment when we met, but which you offered me on the first picture you sent me. I said I would love them by gestures, licking and biting

the erected fleshy nipples, gently and hardly covering them with shining fluid, making you come and scream when I'd rub my too big burning sex upon them. I described my almost fainting with joy when you confessed you had fallen in love with me and my cock, sucking it with so much expertise and intuition it looked like an artistic creation.

From: FB
To: Liz

I want that your so expert lips open on my sex, that your tongue caresses the most sensitive part of my cock, that your hands milk the shaft with love, and that your long lacquered nails gently scrape its length and hardness. When the cum spurts you will drink the first swallow with greediness and the following one will flow all over your face, your belly, your breasts. Do you approve this marvelous love program (among so many others to be described and lived)?

The sex of the other becomes gluttony. Artistic creation. I love so much to suck what is giving me such demonstrative pleasure. The thinness of the skin of his penis is appreciated by my tongue which intrudes into all those parts available to my senses. My mouth slips down his sex and I close my eyes in order to feel full his virility. I like to offer to him the hard contact of my teeth with bites and touches. My hands claim ownership of the places where his seamen burns, curious for sensations, sensitive to his softness and his warmth. I want his pleasure to be intolerable. I'm blocking his orgasm so he can save it to open my intimate entrance glistening with my love juice which flows steadily.

"We can go no further." These were the words that punctuated his orgasm which engendered mine, enclosing his cock with multiple spasms. The room was moved with snorted silences.

From: **FB**
To: **Liz**

You are the most expert love girl I ever met. I will kiss and lick and bite your clit, your tits like no one before, then fill up your pussy and your throat like no other cock before. You will sit on my mouth, on my cock, you will drench them with your mouth and pussy fluids. You will suck as much as you may engulf of my dick, making me feel the length and hardness of your nails on those sensitive spots you know. You will scream with joy when my come jerks into your womb, your throat, covering your breasts and your graceful face. I keep it all just for you, I trust you'll love it.

He slowly pulled the zipper of my dress, gradually exposing my breasts kept in a black silk lace. He honors them with wet and tender kisses that give birth to my approving sighs. I wish once again that he would stop here and stay there longer, but already a precise pressure gives orders to my sex to tear itself open to his mouth and greedy and moist lips. Then I can enjoy the spectacle he offers to me and the acts he lavishes upon me. His caress is intense and profound. I felt a new power. I'm expecting each of his tongue strokes entering into me even more deeply vouchsafing me waves of pleasure. I adore to feel myself like this, completely open and offered to his extremely excited eyes. To die of pleasure. With my eyes closed I feel now his manhood in me. As he stated inordinate desire fills me completely. My mouth let escape a sensual groan as his fluid spread on my belly and my breasts and on my face.

He was once again right. I loved everything . . .

From: FB
To: Liz

While I was not sleeping, nightmarish night, I thought of this very moment when you make love, the ultimate kiss that makes your lover come, just like a specific musical gesture that would bring ultimate pleasure. And I figured — wonder why — you are the keenest expert of this "blue note". My balls are so much filled with sperm that I almost came. I did not, I spare it for you only; you make it spring, it's yours, all.

From: FB
To: Liz

My blue note is to be shared: it means the moment when the ultimate move of yours —your tongue, your nails, your nipples, your sex makes me come. At the very same moment, I offer you the red urge: when your most intimate flesh turns purple with pleasure, having been licked, kissed and fucked by my lips and my cock.

The Blue Note, little words of couple complicity which belong only to the two lovers, exclusive book marks for exclusivity. We had some like that, created by us and only for us. Unique creations which dissolved over time. The writing is fortunately the form which guarantees the memory.

Share of our desire, share of our longing for one another, rebellious impulse. My sex, greedy for him, swollen with vivid heat, swallowed his sex and nothing else existed. The Blue Note was lavished by the symbiotic pitch of our bodies one into the other. My hips transmit a cadenced, addictive and delicious dance. A perfect major chord. I welcome in me his come which caresses my intimate flesh with unqualified delight and he welcomed and discovered my throbbing orgasms which enclosed his cock with rhythmic pressure. A few seconds of simultaneous enjoyment for both of us so idealized and for us realized. Was he conscious of that? It remains in me the untamed scream that accompanied this pleasure.

His tongue over my most intimate flesh: tsunami of pleasure.

Lingering and dragging his cock on my electric, swooning slit. My purple color like an evanescent dusk. A little bit more please my love because it is only in your arms that I'm vibrating in resonance with being me, being you, being us, and nothing else matters. Attainment of nirvana.

From: **FB**
To: **Liz**

You never wrote any of those last two letters to whomever, did you? I will answer accurately, regarding whereabouts, wardrobe, gestures etc. At this very moment, I have one special vision: your erected nipples shining with my bites and kisses jutting out of your black lace bra. I rub them gently with my cock, and you scream with pleasure as you come. And hundreds of other all-exciting love scenes ...

The night is adorning the bedroom with shadows and soft and calming light. I'm waiting for him. My eyes stray to the fake Braque. I'm missing him. My body longs for his languid voice, his hands, his eyes, his kisses. My red lipstick is shining on my lips and becoming impatient.

My lashes bend, inclined to utter the secret contact. I want him here. The door opens ...

My breasts reveal themselves from out of the black embroidered velvet and the long-awaited moist coolness coming from his mouth covers my nipples with declensions of joy. He makes the hatched peaks of my two erect just born rosebuds bloom into an incisive pleasure. My love, lick my pink nipples again and again, bite them and suck them until you make me moan.

His cock is dancing back and forth between my breasts. I adore watching this scene. I admire its size and how he rubs on my skin. I love to watch him and to feel him pant with desire and pleasure. I love his manhood so much. Will he climax here on my breast, on my face, in my mouth? I feel like having everything at the same time. I love so much to have sex with him. I am a volcano who's lava of enjoyment flows between his lips. Only he knows how to make me come like this.

Our mutual sexual love and desire can give birth to hundreds of love scenes. As many as we wish. And all of them will be more than exciting, in the grip of a high flying eroticism that both of us know how to practice. Learn me, my love. Teach me, my love.

SECOND DAY SCHERZO . . .

I learned by heart all these love scenes he evoked so intensely, trying to make everything reality.

The second day, waiting for his return, I adorned myself for him with the greatest care. I took a long, harmonic and sensual bath in candlelight, lulled by the green-orange scent of Hermès, with the bombastic spectacle of a white orchid which was offering me its beauty as an example.

I was relaxing, luxuriating and I was feeling extremely well, forgetting all constraints and mundane reality. Only one fact to focus on — to be the most delicious object of desire I could be. A delightful pleasure of submission which overcomes responsibilities, and makes the thread of life so simple, like slipping into a bubble-bath, or slipping into the skin of a fashion model.

I thought back to the book *The Lover* by Marguerite Duras in which the heroine indicates that she was expecting her lover to possess her like his other women, the prostitutes who were filling his fantasies and desires. As with everything in life, to understand and grasp the concept, one must go through the experience, the empirical. I understood then the words of that lover because love sometimes creates a paradox.

I also thought about his cock in me, and to use a *Grand Siècle* expression, "I swooned" . . .

I knew then what he loved — minimal touches of perfume, very discreet fragrances dissolved or almost imperceptible. The body veiled, half dressed to be browsed and titillate the iris.

My outrageous, skin-tight smoky tights.

Dizzyingly high heels waiting to make their entrance.

Garter sublimating curves.

Thong, black to blend and mingle, to barely cover and to be discovered.

Red silk bathrobe with nipples vehemently piercing the lace.

Lace hair on the immaculate, sweet-sleep inviting white pillow.

Feeling well, magnificently well . . . offered on the huge white bed.

From: **FB**
To: **Liz**

I embrace you.

From: **FB**
To: **Liz**

Your ass is a splendor, which I dream of with envy. I respect without blushing your inclinations, without pretending not to marvel at so exquisite a temptation. You're beautiful, so beautiful, desirable, made to perfection. These are facts that you are aware of. I drink from your swollen breasts, which

are like clusters of voluptuousness. I am enchanted by the extreme tension of your tights and garters on your perfect legs. My thirst is insatiable as I gorge on your intense liquors that your intimacy distills into my mouth. I get drunk on your perfumes, your spirits, the finish of your skin, on your lingerie flooded with pleasure. I want you in black with simple pumps with crazy high heels, black lingerie and black mascara, scarlet lips and long nails. Creating desire and giving pleasure to a woman of your quality is my privilege.

From: FB
To: Liz

I'm sure that you can feel how much my sex is talking to you, that you can guess the volume and the tension of it. You will know like no other how to show me your mastery of the art of love.

I didn't feel the caress immediately, rocked by tender dreams. To awake did not tempt me. Very deeply asleep, his caresses were melting into my erotic dreams. With his long fingers he spread each of my holes to slip, in this order — his eyes, fingers, tongue, cock. I felt a languid and blurry pleasure. I came back to consciousness only when I heard him coming in the place he coveted so much. He was allowed to repeat, in consciousness and in good consciousness, this action as much as he wanted. And he didn't deprive himself of it.

We dozed for a few hours and his sex became full again between my breasts. His supreme liquor spread like a star after I had tasted the first sip. Yes, embrace me again and again, open my flesh with your fingers, make my flesh obsessed with consciousness, tear and rub with your fingers, your mouth, your cock as we watch. I have a passion for you.

My lips parted to make way for his turgid penis that filled

my mouth. It left its aroma and I began to suck with relish. I love it! I scratch its thin skin with my teeth-sweet-bite. My tongue explored the environment with stealthy taps or a long sucking licking and focused on that small hole that touched me so much when I looked at it. I could totally take it in my mouth while my painted nails sank slowly into the parts that remained outside my lips. I know that I know how to suck. He had not yet fully discovered me in this area. I know how to play with everything, with my eyes, my words, my actions and my superlatives that I reserve for the finale. The "Blue Note" mastered to its farthest because I know how to go to the end of the beginning of the enjoyment. Power of women, evidence of deep love.

From: **FB**
To: **Liz**

A sublime gesture that crosses my mind — your beautiful breasts, heavy with desire, stiff peaks highlighted by your purple underwear, laid gently on my eyelids. I feel the infinite sweetness, volume and meaning as I beat my eyelashes on the erect nipples. And when you take them to my lips, they become so big that they fill my sucking mouth and you faint with pleasure. On my cock, grown out of proportion because of your kisses and caresses, you slip the heel of your extreme stilettos touching the most sensitive spot that you have identified. Pure beauty. I take your shoe off your shaded and refined grey stockinged foot, bring it to my mouth, and then delicately caress the open, shiny and hot lips of your femininity and you come again. Fantasy? Yes, of a sensual and aesthetic delight. Claimed. And soon reality, of what you have precisely qualified as supreme voluptuousness — "shared happiness." What do you think?

After a refreshing walk in a nearby park, trees and benches, intimate alcoves, our eyes expressed a mutual and perceptible lust. A light indigenous snack, remarks heavy with emotion, the sun fooling around, brisk walking and architectural eyes. We were going towards what he always called "our bedroom", which delighted me. I was perceiving myself as a guest, but using "our", he made me a partner.

What happened then escaped my full consciousness. With him I experienced "loosing my head", a common expression which became meaningful to me. I will use for guidance his text, because, like all the others expressed up till now, his writing became reality.

He gently laid his eyelids on my breasts. I was wearing, in order to stay the one he loved, high heels, smoked tights, a purple silk teddy which shadowed my body with softened hues. With soft and flowing gestures he slowly slid the thin strap revealing my heavy and begging breasts illuminated by the moonlight. Surprisingly, his eyelids and lashes, but not his look, were placed there and not his greedy lips, which imprisoned and moistened with such art. Another sharp sense of pleasure. I felt an incredible stroke and a gesture of sublime love. The caress of his eyelashes, unlike any other, opened unknown paths for me. Extremely excited by his insistent caresses, I took my breasts with both hands and imposed them in his mouth, eager for a stronger sensation. Finally, his mouth, his so sweet tongue, his soaking saliva, tenfolded my enjoyment. I'm only my breasts which then grew in importance. Half fainting, I lost my senses and almost my consciousness. I am deeply in love with him, with everything and that makes me extremely dizzy. But the most extraordinary was to come, an incredible sexual sophistication.

I wanted again and again to suck his cock. I rubbed my tongue, tickling and expanding on the most sensitive spot, and unexpectedly of the unexpected, he brought my heel there, a surreptitious and furtive gesture, a very symbolic sex symbol. I remembered the noise he made when he took my shoe off my foot, like a gentle hiss with a sense of freedom, not only for my foot but for also for our fantasy. Eyes closed and lascivious, I let myself be curious enough to leave some senses acute. Spread eagle on the edge of the bed, there bloomed a completely unknown feeling which mixed at the same time the moist hardness of my stiletto heels, which he had sucked before to make slippery, and an infinite sensation of sweetness. The stiffness of the leather, whose aroma mixed with the smell of the cream in my pussy, and the tenderness of my intimate flesh, united in a heady marriage of opposites which distilled in me one of the most intense pleasures.

Suddenly the heel was in me, becoming an improvised and burning penis because of my internal desire. I felt also the pressure of his finger on the lips of my sex closing — "mending" he commented — my most secret place on this usurper heel, which offered to him a most exciting vision and made me come infinitely a second time. Oh yes, my love, rub the rigid heel on my softness and push it in me and feel the immense excitation of the spectacle we offer to each other. Supreme delight we were right. Never experienced this before.

Yet, when I read and re-read this email revealing this caress that he invented for us, so different from all that he sent me before, I was incredulous and confused. I have a very open mind, so I can read anything, understand everything, and I think in this case what I understood, not at first, was that this uncomfortable feeling resulting from this email was fed with curiosity and, above all I admit, but that came later, a huge excitement. This described feeling of discomfort was born in me because I became aware of the fact that he knew me better than I knew myself. It was not at all an uncomfortable feeling dictated by modesty, such as I had felt before. Thinking about it further, his perfect knowledge of himself and his tastes and inclinations married mine in an absolute symbiosis.

He kept on telling me, "What do you think?" This interrogation was given with a complicitous wink, both frivolous and conniving, after the seriousness of the concept of "supreme delight — shared happiness".

It was my perceptions of his conceptions that provided him everything he wanted. However, I kept in my mind and in my soul the certitude of the expression "end of the movie", end of his roles in the play, end of his roles as the "I".

Nevertheless, I also know with certitude that we can go further in our email and sexual relationship, going through all the other forms of relationships existing between a man and a woman. We have everything in our hands.

There exist two meanings to the words "to live". One, in a satin organdy during Arabian nights. The other, in a toothpaste tube and a coffee cup during a rainy day. We need to know, or rather to choose, how to go with happiness from one to the other.

Jean Renoir wrote, "The only things that are important in life are those which we remember." He told me those three days will be unforgettable.

So . . .

I exist still in the life of *One Thousand and One Nights* and in the life of a rainy day.

But above all we existed and we will exist in the absolute time line where those life moments are inscribed forever. That year, that month, that day, that hour, that minute, that second in that place, he and I lived together shared moments that nothing, that nobody can modify. That they remain in the memory or not does not matter. They are eternal in the universe . . . And in my heart.

ULTIMATE DAY . . .

He thought sometimes to shock me by his words. To shock me? I then took the measure of how, despite the exchange of several months, he had given me little time to go further in the discovery of the lover hidden in me. He had obviously sensed it, but he didn't go down that road.

And yet nothing makes me more alive than being physically eager and intellectually in love. The two intertwine to wake up the unexpected volcano which erupts in my heart.

Senses on alert—all of them—and sophistication . . .

I am an Épicurian to the tip of the *accent aigu* and to the dot on the "i". And above all a woman with integrity to the pinnacle of the moan. At climaxing, I am an expert, to make come I have a great mastery. Regarding love, I want myself to be an exception. He didn't experience it. Too short. To savor is a synonym of "to take your time". A very rare commodity.

Consequently, this last and third day, I wanted to make it unforgettable. Never would he have between his hands a sexual alter ego of my ilk.

To be alive to the tips of my nipples, my clit, my lips — absolutely all of them — my fingers, my eyelashes, and every square millimeter of my skin to be exploited for a gentle swoon.

Pooh to submission. Today, I'm dictating the rules . . .

I want a soft and diffuse light which makes the skin glow and our looks radiant. That's when he will embrace me. Complicity of the light in the eyes. A voyeuristic effect.

I want shattering and voluptuous music like the sexual act, having my favorite Japanese pianist with his traditional instrument — very unexpected modern music with a breathtaking sensuality. With muted pauses which give way to outbreaks of erotic and lustful thoughts, especially created for the instant of us.

I want to drink — champagne and his favorite alcohol in order for him to drink me from the source of my skin. I want ice cream in order for him to suck me cold and hot. And strawberries to mouth share. And some tea for a fellatio he will never forget.

I want the utmost of the suggested caresses.

I want burgundy silk sheets that electrify the skin and reflect it in a burst of whiteness.

There are as many men as ways to fuck. I wanted him at the top level, beyond all that I have known before. I will know how to make him crazy and merry with pleasure, only for me, to savor the fruit of it.

I want the evening, the borning night. I want him in the bedroom dressed with lots of care and style. I want the curtains half open revealing the city below and raindrops gently dripping on the windows.

I want to be in street clothes like I usually am — sophisticated shoes with high heels, black tights with light patterns on my shapely legs, mini black suede skirt and black cashmere Vneck sweater, long earrings, hair at liberty, subtle smile, and a colored scarf.

I want to show off, to offer him a striptease that, because of my knowledge of African and belly dances, will be voluptuous. Pure sensuality just to look at me. Then to dive into a hot bath where he's dressed and I'm naked. He will look at me like the first time he discovered me. That look still haunts me.

I want him to dress me with these little ultra-feminine things — a reverse striptease — with his fingers on my skin, contrary to the natural order.

I want him to adjust my nylons, to slip my underwear all along my flesh. Clumsily perhaps, but for me it will generate the most subtle charm.

I want him to whisper to me all that he is going to do to me with bold, raw and tender words, to spur my eroticism.

And then, I would describe to him the power of his words, the power of his caress, of his gestures, of his love, and of his cock.

To tell him that for me everything is frozen. I'm only feelings. I have this ability to feel in the extreme. A kiss is for me experienced at an exponential power of thousands compared to everybody else. I went deep into suffering and the benefit and the gain from that is that I'm going as far into pleasure and enjoyment.

I want the nighttime stretched, devoted to Love, and everything else set aside.

I want infinite kisses, playing with our tongues and fingers. I want champagne all over my body and to experience the delight as he licks it, his tongue becoming the ultimate tool for my enjoyment. The burn of the alcohol on my sex, quickly followed by his ointments and fluids.

I want to suck his cock with indescribable pleasure, alternating hot tea and mint ice cream to provide the extreme limits, ending with the water of my mouth that will not let him come.

I want unusual hugs issued from his unusual imagination or drawn from his previous experiences that I would never have thought of. It is his turn to invent for our pleasure. I will be a doll in between his fingers ready for everything.

I want bites and gentle touches. I want the hardened tips of my breasts to disappear in his mouth and be titillated by his tongue. I want to sit on his mouth, in order to offer all the things of his fantasies, and to see his eyes on me.

I want words and words. I want him to demand things and I want him to take me there with strength and gentleness.

I will know how to demand things from him too.

I want him to satisfy me, so that I can describe his sex and his sperm in me. I want him to understand my pleasure and discover suitable places on my body. I want to have the power to tell him everything and to ask him anything.

I want him to devour me, as a fire, as a book, as a dish, as a movie. Total fusion only for one night. Unforgettable.

So it was . . .

Sometimes I have to believe in life that does not always believe in me, since a life is growing inside me. Miracle of passion.

"Cosa mentale" as we say in my country, echoing Leonardo. To create you need first an extreme emotion that messes up body and soul. This emotion takes place over all contingencies. I am an artist. I know what breeds creativity. With him, the word passion greatly expanded. Too bad he doesn't believe in it. Me, I know. "It's not because something is unbelievable that it doesn't happen." Our history and its outcome perfectly reflect this statement made by a famous writer.

In fact, whenever certain memories distill themselves in my brain in the form of evocative and moving images, I have to convince myself that this really happened, that my life has taken this turn, that absolutely nothing has predisposed it, except perhaps a whim of fate. But I loved living it so much!

ANALYSIS CHAPTER
WITHOUT ANY SURPRISE

The analysis of my experiences about love and relationships shows that the exact same pattern prevails. A commitment — marriage or living together — made when one is young, dictates the behavior that one will have to keep and maintain throughout life, especially when children are involved. It becomes immoral and unworthy when you want to deviate from the defined path. Divorce exists, but it is destructive, leaves a taste of ashes and bitterness and, above all, does not avoid the fact that children will be shared for a lifetime. I rarely saw couples manage this situation intelligently. Too much rancor. Divorce, separation achieved, what conclusions remain — the need to make enormous personal sacrifices in order to overcome the situation or to become selfish — guilty to others and guilty in one's own eyes? The guilt we inflict on ourselves is very incisive, like the teeth of a rodent, and often becomes a self-destructive, lethal weapon. However, those who handle and deal dexterously with guilt, understanding the ulterior motives lurking behind guilt, are able to overcome who they want. They are also perfectly capable of leading and manipulating other's behaviors according to their own will, without being too obvious.

I also denounce this false morality in which we are submerged from our earliest childhood through stories that could not be more mystifying in their moralistic portrayal of love and marriage for life and their exclusivity. "The beautiful Prince Charming, faithful and flawless." "They married and had many children . . ." This is the end of the fairy tale, where we subtly avoid what follows. Manipulation and control summarize my thoughts about it.

Love is born of an attraction between female and male, or male and female, to engage in what is required by biology. Procreation is the only engine of the sexual act. I speak, of course, in a basic animal context. It is obvious that the complexity of the human brain embroiders many embellishments to that. However, it is undeniable that we obey the laws of biological love. Love allows you to lose your common sense, to idealize the partner, to want his or her presence forever. Forever, a temporal concept which in its extremism shows that it is utopian. A few years are enough, just enough for the new created being, so fragile at birth, that he or she needs two adults to take care of him or her. Hence the popular imagery of the crisis of couples in their seventh year. Seven years for the child is the age for the onset of autonomy. Then, the attention can be focused elsewhere. Another conquest to fertilize. That's why the notion of a couple for life doesn't exist. Love certainly has many different faces, but sex is the mistress and dictates its fancies. So when morality gets involved, and when we try to keep on, we deny our impulses. A natural impulse, a pleonasm, but I'm using the word "natural" scientifically.

The multiplication of terms referring to the same status — marriage, concubinage, civil unions — is proof of our musings on the subject and demonstrates its inadequacy for our contemporary society. In my opinion, when one wants to get out of this moral contract of marriage, and cannot do it because of the pressure of the society, it becomes an attack on individual freedom. The social pressure hinders even the desire to fly to freedom. Too "messy". The couple's relationship follows a path more than difficult. In face of such difficulties, we surrender, trivialize separation, and start a new family.

Then we substitute. I think that evasion, escape, facing the abrupt reality of the couple, is inevitable. Work, travel, writing, art, religion, alcohol, drugs, psychological therapy, etc. — so many obsessional crutches try to restore the balance to which we cling and hang. We are functioning in erroneous areas so we must find the truth elsewhere.

I allow myself to narrate some of my last loving experiences (with other lovers) because I became aware that they obey the same parameters and then become commonplace and expected.

Andrew escapes into his work and above all into music. He has a very unsatisfactory love life which curiously follows exactly the same stereotype that I met so many times before — a very depressive wife who, consciously or not, weaves a cage with the threat of guilt, which beyond imprisonment implies its consequences — castration, a supreme pledge of allegiance. Despite our long time strong and mutual attraction and feelings which he revealed to me, Andrew, after having tasted the temptation, and measured its danger, dives into his movie work and his love for music. He mastered this subject in an unmatched way, devoting so much time and interest to it. I always have news from him, from time to time, because he hasn't been able to forget me.

We think that men are very selfish. Certainly very true, but a necessary evil in order to protect the species. It comes from the reptilian brain. But I don't want to go too far into this thought as it is not the subject of this book. However, I find women egocentric, self-centered and possessive and able to do everything, even wickedness — another atavistic, ancestral behavior — not to be emotionally or physically abandoned. Then follows a chess game, and often the queen is victorious. Beyond love, the highest pinnacle of noble sentiment, is the proclaimed love of the other which is claimed in return, kneaded with the impetuous and self love necessary for survival. Then, beyond love, erected like a dictator who cannot be ignored, rises the anxiety of competition that can become dangerous and damaging. In the first place for self-esteem. One of the many aspects of jealousy is that it involves a lack of confidence, especially when occurs the loss of an asset that has been set in stone, a husband or a wife. But, deeper than that, the anguish of the loss of security and the necessity to fully assume a loneliness and failure, having lost what society considers an end in itself — a successful family life, a single pattern offered and accepted — that blends into the landscape of life and does not confess its faults.

I only mention my experiences, my personal observations and thoughts and I don't apply them systematically to the relationships between men and women, which are currently undergoing a significant revolution orchestrated over many years, but slow to overcome the whirlwind of change.

Théo escapes into traveling and refuses to let his young child be a hindrance to the life he has chosen to pursue. But, acutely aware of the innocence of his son, he compensates by giving him most of his free time. Despite our complicity, our laughter, our agreement on many topics and also feelings, his free time is not inexhaustible. He runs around the world with a camera in his hands and thus he is not often around. He refuses to be tied down and juggles a very stressful schedule and a disjointed family life, but he cannot entirely be blamed for this, even if he is reproached with hints of guilt and bitterness. I always have news from him from every part of the world and I'm writing our history. I know he hasn't forgotten me.

A question: in such circumstances is it still possible for them to experience feelings and desire for the woman who is sharing their life? I truly believe that yes, after having had many discussions with them.

Him, he escapes in travels, real or in thought, and in work. He possesses a great emotional intelligence and a very refined and demanding sexuality. As a result, he is subject to an equally extreme sensitivity that causes him confusion. He remains for me unique. Only a man of his exceptional sensitivity was able to provide the stimuli in order to satisfy both my own demanding sexuality and my intellect.

The more I read what he wrote to me, and the more I look back on our shared moments, the more I sink into a kind of certainty that told me he was sincere. Healing balm? Whatever, I love this certainty. But he is stuck in his real life. I was just a small breath of fresh air and an outlet for his deep sentimental nature. Sort of a small parentheses for his dreams and to realize his hidden impulses. What did his last look at the door of the hotel room mean? "I am sorry but I have to abandon you here." Here, an adverb including both place and time.

However . . .

YES, FOR HIM I WILL BE SOFT LIGHT AND PERFECT IDYLL. HE WILL COME TO MY ISLAND'S ENCHANTING SHORES, VOLUPTUOUS CURVES, WHERE WILL BE BORN BLUE OSMOSIS. I HAVE A TATTOO OF TWO ELEGANT LETTERS AND I FEEL LIKE AN ORGY OF KISSES. THERE IS NOTHING BETTER IN MY LIFE THAN WHEN I SEX WITH HIM.

I remain confident that we can love each other perfectly. So I leave it to fate. This book is both my reply and my supplication. But, he nevertheless should be aware of :

I AM A TATTOO
SUBLIMATED WITH INK
ONCE CALLIGRAPHED
NOTHING CAN ERASE ME.

These last men in my life have one thing in common, they finally preferred the family foundations, even if they suffer in their emotional and sexual life. They try to feel the best they can, trying to hide and conceal everything from themselves. A novel comes to my mind, *I Loved Him* by Anna Gavalda.

Although my requests to them are light and mild, they nonetheless hesitate, not taking any risk that could lead them to any kind of trouble or unpleasantness in the world or in themselves. They quickly perceive the danger I represent, because it is easy to love me and also, according to what they say — and I respect their words word for word — I am about sex: "a hyper turn-on; a total hallucination; too good; exquisite incarnated temptation; expert; so sweet; such a beautiful embodiment of desire; the more I make love to you, the more I want you; Liz, my head, my heart and my body work hard for you; etc." Expressions I saved intact, keeping in mind the different generations and French not always being their mother tongue. I am a danger so they avoid me. A cruel paradox that I have to face and that I have experienced so often.

And why duplicate what was a mistake the first time. After some time the result will be exactly the same. What is more unconquerable than feelings of love and desire? They will fall on you and leave you just as suddenly, without warning. So, let's behave properly according to the morality of the society, preserve the family, jostle absolutely nothing, and live or not live a few moments of good time that do not have any consequences. Perfectly understandable and plausible. But, with another open mind and another way of looking at love and possessiveness, how many tragedies could be avoided or at least softened? There are other ethnicities in far away places, eastern China for example, based on matriarchy that live in peace as they accept shared partners chosen by the women. Have they understood and assimilated the essence of mankind better than us?

I pay dearly for my difference, my differences, having also to be content with a few good times, when possible. Then I repeat my experiences again and again with the same naive hope when I realize that they have an absolutely identical format. Hence their emptiness now because I have been around. They have filled for a time my adventurous nature and my need to learn and to understand. And they have revealed to me also my resistance to commitment and my fear of what is definitive. It is time to move to another level. Since him, I feel ready now for a real commitment.

Might he one day follow me on these roads? . . .

I make this proposition to him because I know from experience that life doesn't pass the dishes twice. This is the joker card of our game that I'm giving him. I believe in an agreement of head and sex between two people — the irrational and mysterious attraction being the first fruits and the challenge. But it is necessary not to be trapped in the forgetting of one's self or in the spiral of renewal constantly renewed.

Our mutual need for such an adventure tells me two things — we are alike in an enormous number of ways and we were at the same point of dissatisfaction in our lives. Our deep love and desire of love and desire being not at all met, although we are both made to honor them with dignity. This is the anchor of our irresistible attraction beyond our consciousness. It grabbed our unconscious as it was screaming with an emptiness to be filled and which vibrated in unison when we met. I now have the explanation of our mutual intense attraction and I know I'm not mistaken.

I regret that other meetings never happened because I'm sure of the uniqueness and the sublimity of our sexual love and the experiences that we could have lived then, now that we know more intimately our bodies, our strengths and weaknesses. He also observed, "Have you noticed that we are making love better and better each time?"

Another fact, biology was not wrong in choosing us for each other. We created what we were designed for. Although difficult to understand in view of the contexts, and yet the truth.

Looking back, I can now say exactly when this union, what is called scientifically "fertilization", occurred. I'm listening to myself and my inner self as I am listening to other people. While waiting for my flight whose departure was delayed because of a storm, I was feeling a kind of enjoyable drowsiness that led me to a gentle sleepiness. I felt perfectly well in this state of semi-sleep that I attributed to our recent acts of love, and far away from what was happening in my body. I noticed, however, the uniqueness of these feelings which did not reflect me at all. I'm always in a state of absolute control, especially in public places and regardless of how tired I am. My deep instinct for survival.

From: **FB**
To: **Liz**

How can I understand your narcissistic dizziness, this mirror that you hold and that you share with a chosen few. By the way, why me? Who, unlike you, greatly doubts himself. You'll respond again to me, won't you?

How I could feel his suffering in this non acceptance of his appearance. While I admired his hands, full of character and beautiful, he had this following reflection, "This is probably the best thing I possess." This pinched my heart. In bed, he expressed how much he regretted offering me only a bony body in the face of soft and comfortable curves. I wanted to tell him how I did not care and whatever else he offered me was so delicious. However, the acute awareness that he developed about his physical details, reflected a deep and long suffering. Not accepting oneself physically must be so difficult to live with. But for me he was awesome and I know he would have become even more so because of and for me. He did laugh when I told him that with his physique he could wear young and trendy attire and I honestly thought that. We also had another thing in common — aging had no effect on us. Love of love probably. I thought he had this youthful freshness that did not reflect his age and impacted on his physique. Rare. I loved him a lot for that too.

A little aside just for him. When I translated into French all his writings, putting the translations just below the original words created by his English pen, I then felt something strange. The text flowed along because I was as if directly connected to his brain, his mind, his instincts, his feelings, his emotions, his whole being, his sex and his expressions. So I think that I did not betray any of his statements, because sometimes the bridge leading from one language to another is fraught with cultural-semantic obstacles. I rarely used the dictionary, and when I did it was just because I'm a perfectionist that needed security. This characteristic of mine he noticed and so he was able to understand me.

My analysis and my experience now make me want a relationship which is at the same time based on an agreement where there are no sexual or intellectual constraints and no trade offs. A relationship that also respects the essence of the other and the meaning of his life and his freedom. To enjoy the present moment to its utmost, keeping in mind that love is fickle. A relationship showing absolute sharing, tolerance, compassion and understanding. I redundantly reiterate and insist in this paragraph what I have already written in order to be deeply rooted, as if to more and more convince both of us. "I know that our commingling will be intellectual and sexual, with sophistication and finesse. I know that a look at each other will suffice. I know that we are identical and complimentary. I know that we will draw strength and energy from each other. I know he will tame me and make me his. I know that even absent we will be present for each other and that our past will forge us strongly, to ground for our future. For him I will be superlative and I will fulfill him and love him."

Although my adventures proved ephemeral and without a follow-up, they all had, in varying degrees however, a taste of passion, fullness, sharing and enjoyment. I refuse to live a chloroformed, mediocre life wrapped in a partnership of appearances. But few of my admirers are confident enough acrobats sufficiently well trained to trapeze with me. I do not despair, however, challenge being my challenge.

I expect my acrobat to catch me before I decline and splatter into the net below . . .

EMOTIONAL CHAPTER
NO LOVE FICTION

All these following emails of his, a witnessed river of five months of untamed passion, are the ones I prefer. They are the ones which kindled my senses, pinched my heart, tyrannized my sex. I deliver them in this last chapter "to feast on them again and again." I like to use his expressions that are engraved in me, as they were unique and beautiful.

From: **FB**
To: **Liz**

You are the crazy irresistible impulsive kind, you know that. I love it, and your décolleté too, I admit. You CAN NOT blame me for that, can you? By the way, you're some sort of an artist, too. So am I. What's next?

From: **FB**
To: **Liz**

You are "magnifique!" So singular and intriguing. I'll pack up a bunch of gentle words just for you. Almost forgot: you're the sexiest I can remember and dream of.

From: **FB**
To: **Liz**

Lovely. I love you in black. And in white also. The first one is ever so sexy, the second ever so tender. This coming new day will be gentle...

From: FB
To: Liz

You wrote you wanted me to express my feelings and desires. I do so, since, in a way, I know you love it too. No claim to shock you. But what could be shocking provided it is sincere, deeply perceived and shared? With you, I feel free to write love words, and not ashamed at all to quote my admiration and dedication for your beauty. You are not your sole body: could you imagine I did not get the essence of your being? Could I plunge right into your heart and sex if I had not captured the truth about Liz? You are a lover that has not been loved accordingly. *A Delicate Balance:* do you remember this play by Edward Albee?

From: FB
To: Liz

Your sweetest kisses reached my inner self. I loved their taste, their depth, their unending wilderness and demand. They plunge into my throat, my spine, my heart, they drive my conscience to obsession. My body is set afire, my cock hurts, begging for your attention. Lovesickness.

From: FB
To: Liz

You are beautiful from everywhere. Yours, all.

From: FB
To: Liz

You are light. You are the most vivid and also the most abstract light. A work of art and flesh. Hauntingly sublime.

From: FB
To: Liz

With you Liz, love is but a poem of words, of gestures, of thoughts. Not only does it bring together all our senses: it also upsets our grounds, making us tumble and swoon in an unknown world of feelings, where past and present mix up with dreams. [...] appears as a beginning as well as a completion, an earthly vision of the utmost. At this moment, the hardest part of me enters the softest part of you, we think we're dying with pleasure. We are.

From: FB
To: Liz

A stormy, rainy day. The type of weather I like most. *Raindrops keep falling on my head*: you remember the song. It's all wet, declining light, wet atmosphere. Landscape blurred. Concentrated on my thoughts and dreams [...] The sexiest, the most dramatic visions I ever gave shelter to haunt my inspiration. I don't remember the way I looked at you, I just recall I could not prevent my eyes to focus on yours. Then, it all started, unless it was begun already but we had no conscience of it yet. Beyond ourselves, beyond our will and wish. What do you think?

From: FB
To: Liz

You fit my dreams, and I'm a dreamer. I want you.

From: FB
To: Liz

You are marvelous. I put my lashes on the tip of your nipples.
Write to me sex love.

From: FB
To: Liz

Carried along by the substantial task I assigned to myself. A
very mind absorbing activity, implying concentration, silence,
time elapsing. Then enters Liz, in my mind, in my heart, in my
body. My sex escapes from my control and conscience, grows
so big and hard, mad with desire and passion, devastating and
aching. I feel I would almost cry. Rescued by literature, and
expectation: your next sexy message, our next wild reunion.

From: FB
To: Liz

Do not change in any respect, please! I love you the way you
are, in every aspect. I hold your breasts to my lips, kiss and bite
the nipples, cover them with shining fluid, stroke them with
the rim of my demanding cock. Your long red painted nailed
hand holds it, press if between your breasts, take it to your lips
and tongue... I almost faint with delight. Would you?
I kiss your sweet lips, mingle our tongues, one of the most
intimate love gestures, don't you think? (With many others
I let you describe, unless we share this delightful task). The
best, the sweetest, the hottest for you.

From: FB
To: Liz

I received the strength of your tenderness. Your extreme
photos are crazily tempting for me. I'm ready to receive them.

To devour them. To adore them. I kiss you — etymologically it is not the right word — I'm drinking the water of life at your mouth.

From: **FB**
To: **Liz**

There is no difference in our feelings, based on an irresistible mutual attraction. I never ever thought I would write down anything like what I just sent you, because I never felt anything like it. Nor did you. When I think of your lips, the upper and the inner ones, I see them as a sacred piece of love I bring to my breath, to dig proper life out of them, my eyes closed, my heart pulsating, actually seeing the inside hidden essence of you, Liz.

"My hidden essence" — the computer had the power to reveal it to him after our hypnotic looks. So I ask myself, what was the role of this fabulous and diabolical tool? A total liberation of our dreams and fantasies that will stay forever defined through all these poetical writings, at the same time erotic and tender, designed in a reassuring solitude, protected by the screen. Or, conversely, an absolute revelation of our deep being undressed and revealed through this tool and screaming about what we want to live and about what we are really . . . Dreams in heaven or earth anchored. In summary, our relationship technologically orchestrated, was it the life of our fantasies or the life of our essences? Or both? Sublime wealth.

FINALE
WINK AND A SMILE
END OF THE ANTHOLOGY

P RESENTER: Ève Winter, you are signing here your third novel which is titled *The Blue Note* and subtitled *Electronic Erotica.* Reading you one might think that this is not really a novel but rather an autobiographical story describing a slice of your quite personal life. Do you agree?

Ève: I prefer to leave that to the readers. Your professionalism tends to categorize it among this type of book. However, I wanted it unclassifiable. The term novel is a generic term that allows this.

P: Then, could you tell us what the title of your novel indicates? I usually don't get hung up on this first revelation of a book, but in this case a certain discordance has brought me to do so.

È: A discordance between the title, the subtitle and the content you are asking? I don't think there is one. But once again I want readers to discover by themselves the real hidden meaning of the "blue note". I wanted the uniqueness of this love and sex story, mediated by the computer, to be orchestrated like a piece of music, both harmonic and discordant like love itself. So we are in accord.

P: In fact the content of the book is unique because it tells something about a love story that began with a look of love at first sight, doesn't it, which takes the form of a mutual discovery by computer — the emails that you reveal to us, and a short rendez-vous in a hotel room. We are expecting an exchange. You rather present his emails almost as a monologue. Why do you frustrate the reader by not revealing her emails?

È: In a way that the reader enters better into the skin of my character, just having a look at the development of the story through his emails. But I find you very unfair because I did allow her a great deal of space to vent her emotions.

P: That's right. We perceive also a strong under-lying emotion that develops slowly and that is reflected throughout this autobiographical story. You will not mind, I hope, that I prefer to use the expression "autobiographical story"?

È: Absolutely not. You are a reader also and you can choose any interpretation you want. Regarding the emotion, in fact I wanted it very present and seen in its various forms. Love is a feeling that I will compare to an antique writing-desk, or rather a chest of seven drawers. Do you know what I mean?

P: Yes. I see that. From the same drawers where your heroine Liz took her love attire, which is what you called her "lingerie". As for the feelings, we are actually sliding down many slopes. The evidence — the suitcase, which speaks to us poorly and humorously, taking the place of the heroine. And also you are playing dexterously with words in order to lower the emotion on one hand, but make it stronger on the other hand. We understand how annoyed and disappointed Liz is, having been first invited, which explains the purchase of the suitcase, then ignored by this man she only knows through the exchange of emails, and which he inexplicably and abruptly stopped. He acted that way to make her understand that he no longer wants to receive her, hence the thrown return of the suitcase to the closet. One sees why this sudden change, but you don't address the issue directly? Why?

È: This is not an important point of the story because she will leave to join this man. I put highlights on the character's feelings and not on what predisposes her to those feelings. I try to lead the reader into the same exponential and multiple spiral she is experiencing.

P: It is successful because we can feel the crescendo into the relationship that, however, is constrained and marked by all these emotions described as negative, such as conflict and jealousy, which this unusual relationship will not escape. In addition, you are stingy with your commas, which hastens the reading. I perceive that as purposeful in order to illustrate this emotional crescendo, isn't that so?

È: Yes, I want to demonstrate that a relationship between a man and a woman, even in a very unusual and rarefied form, is always confronted with the same pitfalls and cannot escape what we all know in our everyday life in a more conventional form. Regarding my stinginess, as you say, of permitting one to catch one's breath, you saw it perfectly. It is designed to betray the emotional.

P: We also understand how much the writing — they communicate very little in speech — sometimes transcends the oral expression, but also how the process is slower and heavier, the understanding not having the support of the look and the tempo of the breathing.

È: Their relationship is in one part virtual, they don't live it in the flesh. They live it in writing, but their goal is to live it in life overcoming all the obstacles because, the sexual factor which, in their case is not fulfilled by the virtual, is going to be preponderant.

P: In fact, you describe this sexuality with precision — the images and the vocabulary are very real and do not drape themselves with modesty. Everything mentioned, I would say, is raw, natural, and blunt. But you wished that the emotion would sometimes be muted.

È: You are forgetting the poetry and the art of the words. Obviously, they know how to write and despite the rawness, as you say, I have tried to raise the sensitivity and the sensual edge to the surface of the skin.

P: I was getting there. You beat me. The beauty of the lewd sexual evocation is not to be denied. The exchanges are very sophisticated in their structure and vocabulary. We can feel a lot of a great writer and his pen. What do you think about that?

È: At the risk of appearing vain, I had such a genius.

P: This novel, well rather, this autobiographical story, ends with an unusual declaration of love coupled with a proposal that couldn't be more clear. Your heroine has guts, I would say, because such an approach is usually offered by men and is very intimate.

È: This is very true. However, I thought my heroine and

this story, as you noticed, absolutely extraordinary in that they demonstrate reality, intimacy and purity at a depth within themselves. This, in my opinion, is the essence of a book that one reads with feeling. I exhibit here, and I choose this word deliberately, life, one life.

P: One last question, why this enameling of musical terms?

È: I am Italian and from a family of musicians. I wanted this to show through. But I also had the idea to make the reader understand that their story was harmonic, melodic and symphonic, since the emails will never have eyes to reflect the soul, or ears to be enchanted by sighs.

www.ingramcontent.com/pod-product-compliance
Lightning Source LLC
Chambersburg PA
CBHW052141070326
40690CB00047B/1341